BY NICK ELIOPULOS

MINECRAFT™
ZOMBIES
RETURN!

MINECRAFT™
ZOMBIES
RETURN!

NICK ELIOPULOS

RANDOM HOUSE

WORLDS
NEW YORK

Copyright © 2023 by Mojang AB. All rights reserved.
Minecraft, the MINECRAFT logo, the MOJANG STUDIOS logo,
and the CREEPER logo are trademarks of
the Microsoft group of companies.

Published in the United States by Random House Worlds,
an imprint of Random House, a division of
Penguin Random House LLC, New York.

RANDOM HOUSE is a registered trademark,
and RANDOM HOUSE WORLDS and colophon are
trademarks of Penguin Random House LLC.

Hardback ISBN 978-0-593-59780-4
International edition ISBN 978-0-593-72413-2
Ebook ISBN 978-0-593-59781-1

Endpaper illustration: Kaz Oomori

Printed in the United States of America on acid-free paper

randomhousebooks.com

2 4 6 8 9 7 5 3 1

First Edition

Book design by Elizabeth A. D. Eno

For my growing family

MINECRAFT™
ZOMBIES
RETURN!

CHAPTER 1

The night was dark and full of hostile mobs.

Ben could hear them, just beyond the light of his torches. He heard shuffling footsteps, the clatter of bones, and in the distance, a low, inhuman moan.

Every instinct told Ben to turn around, to go back inside . . . to run away from those eerie nocturnal noises.

Instead, he moved toward them.

Ben shuddered with fear as he left his small circle of light. The light was cast by torches that he'd placed all around his modest shelter. The squat, stone-and-dirt dwelling was not at all impressive. But in the warm yellow hues of the torchlight, it was like a bright and welcoming island in a sea of darkness.

Ben hated to leave his little oasis. But even without the torches, he could see well enough. The moon overhead was bright, and the plains stretched out all around him with only the occasional tree to block his view. With a bit of luck—and some skillful sneaking—he would be able to avoid the monsters that prowled the night.

He saw red eyes glowing up ahead. They were the eyes of a spider on the hunt. He crouched low and stopped moving; he stayed completely still. He watched, for a moment, to learn if the red eyes were watching him back. But they moved haphazardly, drifting off to the west.

Ben went east.

It wasn't that Ben was helpless. He had survived his fair share of fights. He was equipped with an iron sword, a shield, and iron armor—not the *best* equipment he'd ever used, but good enough to give him the upper hand against any Overworld mob he might encounter.

But on a night like tonight, on an open plain like this one, a battle would draw too much attention. Ben might easily be outnumbered and overwhelmed. He was better off staying low and quiet and avoiding fights, if he could.

This had all been a lot easier when he'd had a partner. But things were different now. These days, Ben was less an adventurer . . . and more a babysitter.

And he hadn't been doing a *great* job of that.

"Johnny?" he whispered. "Johnny, are you out here?"

As if in response, that low moaning sounded again, closer than before. Ben peered into the gloom, scanning the horizon. In the middle distance, he saw the outline of a humanoid figure. He couldn't see much detail in the moonlight, but he could see the outstretched arms and the sickly greenish hue of the skin.

It was a zombie. But was it the zombie Ben was looking for? Ben crept closer before speaking again. "Johnny, is that you?"

A growl was his answer. A growl—and a mindless, vicious lunge.

Ben acted instinctively, jumping back while slashing his sword ahead of him. The move kept him out of the zombie's reach, even as the creature took damage.

At melee range, by the light of the moon, he could clearly see that this was *not* the zombie he was looking for. Which was lucky for him, actually—he was supposed to keep Johnny safe, not hit him with a sword.

This zombie, however? This zombie he could fight to his heart's content.

Ben lunged, slashed, then stepped back, careful to always stay out of the mob's reach. After avoiding trouble for so long, it felt *good* to let loose.

But he was rusty. Ben misjudged the timing of his final lunge, and the zombie's clawed swipe struck him in the chest. Ben stumbled back. Even through his chest plate, he felt a flare of pain.

"So rude!" he said, slashing out with his sword. The zombie collapsed, defeated, and left behind a scrap of rotten flesh. Ben knew it was edible, and his food supplies were running low. But he wasn't *that* desperate. Not yet.

Nearby, another groan sounded. It was just as he'd feared; the battle had drawn unwanted attention. Ben whirled around, sword raised—

And just barely stopped himself in time.

"Johnny!" he said. "I nearly cut you in half. Bad baby!"

The mob standing before him was, in fact, a baby . . . but not a typical one. Johnny had been attacked during a zombie siege and transformed into one of the undead. His skin was green, his eyes shone red beneath a heavy black brow, and his clothes were dirty and tattered. He also wore a lead, which Ben reached for immediately.

Johnny growled and snapped at Ben's hand.

"Hey! No!" said Ben. "Just because your sister isn't here doesn't mean it's back to bitey-bitey. Behave yourself."

Johnny growled again, but it was a low, quiet growl that sounded to Ben almost like an apology.

Or maybe a growl was just a growl, and Ben had been spending far too much time in the company of zombies.

Ben had encountered plenty of zombie villagers before, and those encounters usually ended in a fight—one that only Ben walked away from. But a strange and special bond had developed between him and Johnny. It helped that Johnny's big sister, Bobbie, had somehow been able to teach him basic manners.

When they first met, Bobbie had hired Ben to help her find a cure for her brother's condition. But they'd become separated—and the last thing Bobbie had said to Ben was that it was *his* responsibility to keep her brother safe.

Ben liked responsibility about as much as zombies liked sunlight. Which reminded him . . .

"We need to go back home," Ben said, and this time he grabbed Johnny's lead without any complaint from the young zombie. "The sun will be up soon. So unless you want to wear your special hat . . . ?"

Ben held out a carved pumpkin. When worn as a helmet, it kept Johnny protected from the sunlight, but the baby absolutely hated wearing it. As soon as he saw it, he growled and grumbled, pulling on the lead as if trying to get away.

"Okay, I'm putting it back in my inventory!" said Ben. "But that means we need to go back to the house right now. Bobbie will never find us if we stray too far. And she'll definitely never forgive me if you catch fire. I might feel a little bad about it, too."

At the mention of his sister's name, Johnny emitted a low, mournful growl. He pulled again at his lead, but softly this time. He wasn't trying to escape Ben's grasp—he was trying to lead him across the plain.

"So that's why you wandered off," said Ben. "You miss your sister, is that it? You want to go find her?"

Johnny's growl sounded almost like a purr.

"Sorry, buddy," Ben told him. "The Overworld is too big. She could be anywhere." He shook his head. "We have to stay where we are and trust that *she* will find *us*."

Johnny almost seemed to be sulking on the walk back to their shelter. He dragged his feet, ignoring Ben's whispered requests to hurry up. Of course, Johnny had nothing to fear from the night. The monsters of the Overworld recognized him as one of their own; whereas they recognized Ben as a potential meal. A tasty one!

"We're almost home," Ben whispered. "We'll get a good night's rest, and then things will look better in—ooh, treasure!"

Even in the face of danger and uncertainty, Ben was an adventurer at heart. And adventurers loved loot. "A little detour won't hurt," he reasoned.

Ben hadn't walked this path before. What he'd thought, at a distance, was a simple tree turned out to be an arc of stone and obsidian. It looked almost like a portal, but an incomplete one— or perhaps one that had fallen into disrepair. He didn't have the tools to harvest the obsidian, but there was a chest tucked up against the structure. Whatever it contained was his for the taking.

Ben lifted the lid, and when he saw the glint of gold, his heart soared. For a moment, he thought he'd found a golden apple— a key ingredient in the cure they needed for Johnny.

But he was wrong. It wasn't a golden apple within the chest, but a golden carrot.

"Maybe it works the same?" he wondered out loud, and he held it out for Johnny to take a taste. The zombie boy swatted the gold-plated vegetable away.

"Yeah, probably not," said Ben, and he stashed the carrot in his inventory.

After they left the ruined portal behind, it was easy to find their shelter. On a night like this one, its lights were visible at a great distance.

As they reentered the glow of the torches, Ben felt a rush of relief. He allowed himself to feel safe again. He stopped looking over his shoulder for fear of an ambush.

He had dropped his guard too soon.

Torchlight stopped new monsters from spawning. But it didn't always keep away the monsters that already prowled the night. And one monster had found its way to the shelter. As it rounded the corner and came into view, it made its presence known . . . with a sudden, urgent *hisssssss*.

"Creeper!" cried Ben. "Get back!"

Ben put himself between the creeper and Johnny, shoving the zombie boy to safety as the creeper exploded. Ben felt the impact all along his iron-armored back, but he managed to stay on his feet. If he'd been any slower, both he and Johnny might have been eradicated. They'd been lucky this time.

"Are you okay?" Ben asked, and Johnny grumbled.

Ben turned to examine the damage done by the creeper's explosion. It was extensive. Fully half of their shelter had been blown away, and Ben's meager belongings—the resources he'd been able to gather during the daylight and then stash in a simple wooden chest—had been scattered all over the ground. Where the creeper had stood, there was now a hole in the ground, and the nearest torches had been blown away, their light snuffed out. More monsters might appear at any moment.

"This is hopeless," Ben said. "I don't have the materials I need to make a better shelter." He turned to look at Johnny. "And I can't keep an eye on *you* and mine resources at the same time."

Ben peered into the hole the explosion had made. Beneath the ground, he could see the mine cart tracks that had brought him here. He remembered where that track led.

"But I know where we can find a real shelter." He grinned, then turned to clap Johnny on the shoulders. "Logan's not using his fortress anymore. How about you and I move in?"

Johnny tried to bite Ben's hands, and he quickly pulled them away.

He was pretty sure that was Johnny's way of saying: *Good idea, Ben. You're the best. Lead on!*

CHAPTER 2

Far away and on the move, Bobbie had problems of her own.

Sunlight was a distant memory, and sleep was a foreign concept. She'd been on her feet, marching in a dark subterranean tunnel for . . . she didn't know how long. How long had it been since she'd been separated from Ben and her brother? How long since she'd decided to follow their foe as he marched at the head of his army into the darkness? She didn't know the answer.

Not that there was anyone to ask her. Bobbie was alone — truly alone, for the first time in her life.

She thought of her brother. She remembered him as he had once been: a charming, sometimes frustrating, rambunctious little baby who enjoyed jumping on beds and collecting flowers from the village golem. And then she remembered him as he was now: green-skinned, half wild, prone to biting. A zombie. And it was all because of the bottomless greed of one person: an adventurer named Logan.

Logan was ahead of her in this very tunnel. The only thing standing between Bobbie and her foe . . . was about three hundred zombies.

Maybe it was only two hundred. Bobbie hadn't had a chance to actually count them. All she knew was there were a lot of them. Logan had gathered them from all over, trapping wild zombies and then using those zombies to infect villagers. Bobbie had seen it firsthand. She'd watched as her own family, friends, and neighbors had been transformed—infected—just as her brother had been. And now they were among the great horde of undead creatures that Logan was leading through this massive, seemingly endless tunnel, on their way to . . . *somewhere*. Nowhere good, Bobbie figured.

Even as Bobbie followed, she kept her distance. If the zombies discovered her—if they turned around and attacked en masse—she wouldn't last for long against their numbers. And she had no idea how astute a zombie's senses might be. Could they smell her if she got close? Could they see her in the dark? She didn't know.

So she had to be careful. Cautious. But above all, she couldn't let the zombies get away. If they got away, she might never find them again.

And then her friends and neighbors would be lost to her forever.

A sound went up, echoing up and down the great tunnel. It

wasn't the groan of a zombie this time—those came frequently enough; this was the sound of a goat horn. She knew by now that it was the signal to stop marching and rest. And that meant she was about to have company.

Bobbie looked around for a hiding spot, but this section of tunnel had been carved out by human hands. There were no alcoves or stalagmites to hide behind, just smooth, regular walls. She would have to make her *own* hiding spot, and quickly.

Armed with a pickaxe, she made short work of the stone wall, cutting a narrow hole just one block wide, two blocks tall, and three blocks deep. She stepped inside it and replaced one of the stones she'd just cut away, so that she was half hidden and obscured in shadow. She'd be very difficult to spot, while she would still have a view of whatever happened next.

She watched as a fast-moving figure emerged from the darkness. He stayed just beyond the reach of the horde of zombies as he dropped fencing all around them. It was far too dark to see in detail, but Bobbie could guess that he was trembling with fear. He wore a full set of leather armor, and he clearly knew it would not be enough to keep him safe if the horde got their hands on him.

The figure was named Ben. But he wasn't *her* Ben—not the friend she'd left behind to watch her brother. This was a boy she thought of as "Other Ben." He was Logan's so-called "squire"— more like his servant, really—and it was his job to keep the zombies moving in the right direction. That meant luring them forward with turtle eggs during the day and laying down a barrier to keep the mobs from wandering off at night.

It must be night, then, Bobbie reasoned. And she was certainly tired enough to rest. She watched as Other Ben hurriedly set the last piece of fence into place, connecting it to the stone wall. The leather helmet slipped around on his head, and he had to keep moving it back into place.

"Dude, what is taking so long?" That was Logan, rounding the makeshift fence with a look of irritation on his face. He was wearing armor, too, but it was made of diamond. His helmet fit him perfectly.

"I'm done!" said Other Ben. "The fence is all finished!"

"It's about time," said Logan. "And don't forget to pack it all up in the morning, right? Wood doesn't grow on trees, you know."

"Yeah, I know," said Other Ben.

Logan chortled. "Uh, wood *does* grow on trees. That was a joke. Lighten up, kid."

Logan smacked Other Ben in the back in a way that looked almost friendly. But it was a harder hit than it needed to be. Other Ben winced, and his helmet tilted askew.

"Get dinner ready, all right? I'm starving," Logan said, and he turned to head back to the front of the horde.

Bobbie watched from her hiding place as Other Ben sighed. He righted his helmet, then set down a bed, a furnace, and a chest.

Bobbie wished she could do the same. She briefly considered digging a bit deeper, carving out a proper room for herself, with space for a bed. But the danger of oversleeping was too great. What if Logan's army was gone when she woke? How could she be certain she'd catch up to them again?

In the end, she decided she couldn't risk sleeping. Nor could she risk lighting a furnace—the fire might draw unwanted attention. So it would be a cold dinner again, and a long night, punctuated with the moans and groans of the nearby horde.

One thing was sure: The sounds of that many zombies, just a few blocks away, were eerie enough to prevent her from dozing off.

As she settled in for the night, her eyes drifted again to Other Ben. He was organizing his belongings, moving some items to the simple wooden chest. When he pulled a turtle egg from his inventory, the nearby zombies went wild, straining to reach past the wooden fence. Other Ben jumped back, as if uncertain whether the fence would hold. He quickly put the egg away.

Bobbie didn't know why, but zombies really had it in for turtle eggs. They would go out of their way to smash them.

That was how Logan kept his undead army on the march. They followed the turtle eggs . . . which Other Ben, frightened out of his wits, carried just out of their reach.

Bobbie found that interesting.

"I think I'm *hatching* a plan," she whispered to herself, and she chuckled at her own pun. Then, sighing, she thought: Ben—*her* Ben—would have laughed at that one.

CHAPTER 3

Ben would have preferred to travel aboveground, in the light of the sun.

But Johnny didn't want to wear the carved pumpkin helmet that would protect him from the harmful rays of sunlight. (Not that Johnny had said so out loud. But the gnashing and slashing gave Ben a pretty strong impression of Johnny's opinion on the subject.) And traveling aboveground at *night* invited all sorts of problems. If Ben got into a fight, would Johnny help out, as he had when his sister had been around? Would Ben have to worry about keeping his young charge safe in the midst of chaos? Or would the zombie boy take the opportunity to slip away from Ben and disappear into the night?

In the end, it was no choice at all. Ben and Johnny would have to travel by tunnel. It was a tunnel they'd traveled once before. Fortunately, there were torches to prevent hostile mobs from spawning . . . and a rail track that would lead them right to their destination.

"There could be all sorts of riches right beneath our feet, you know," said Ben. "Emeralds and redstone and diamond ore. Stuff I could use to make better gear." He held up an iron pick-axe. "Maybe we should make a little detour? Dig around and see what we can find?"

"Grawr," said Johnny.

Ben sighed. "I wish you could talk. Even if just to disagree with what I was saying." He grinned. "Your sister disagreed with me all the time! It got on my nerves sometimes. But it was better than walking in silence."

"Marr!" said Johnny.

"Silence might be better than the inhuman noises, though," Ben replied.

Although Ben had suggested it, he didn't dare make a mining detour. There was the obvious problem—digging deeper meant more danger—but aside from that, if Ben lost the railway, he might never find it again. And if that happened, he probably wouldn't be able to find Fort Rot.

Logan—Ben's traitorous partner, former friend, and current least favorite person—had built the fortress, as well as the extensive series of tunnels that led to it. Both were key aspects of his mad ambitions to raise an army of the undead. Ben and Bobbie had attempted to put a stop to the whole thing, but they'd been separated, with Bobbie staying behind in the hope of following

Logan and curing the zombies. She'd sent Ben and Johnny to safety in a high-speed automated mine cart, entrusting her zombified sibling to Ben's care.

When the mine cart had finally come to a stop, Ben had built a small structure aboveground and surrounded it with enough torches to make it a beacon, visible from a great distance. He had assumed Bobbie would return to them, and he wanted to stay where she would be certain to find them.

But many days had passed, with no sign of her. As Johnny grew more restless, Ben grew more concerned. What had Bobbie gotten herself into? What could possibly keep her away from her brother, whom she loved so dearly? How could she hope to thwart Logan without the help of Ben, who had far more combat experience than she did and had seen pretty much every biome the Overworld had to offer?

Ben was pondering these questions as he and Johnny approached the end of the tunnel.

"Well, that's new," Ben said. He'd expected to be able to enter the fortress directly from the tunnel, but a wall had been built—a lustrous black blockade at the tunnel's mouth. "Obsidian," he said, running a hand along the super-tough material. "And all I've got is an iron pickaxe. Which will be slow—and loud. I don't know about you, but I'd rather not announce our presence just yet." He looked at Johnny. "We'll have to go up. Unless you have another idea?"

"Gaaar," said Johnny.

"I assume that means it's unanimous," said Ben. "Up we go."

It was simple enough to build a basic staircase and cut through the stony ceiling of the tunnel. As luck would have it, night had fallen; while Johnny would burn up in the sun, he had nothing to fear from moonlight.

Ben, on the other hand, felt a shudder of fear as he emerged onto the surface. Logan's fortress loomed over him, as imposing as it had ever been, with its red-and-black skull-and-crossbones banner and zombie heads placed on posts. The heads were blank-eyed, staring out at the surrounding plateau and seeing nothing.

Ben covered Johnny's eyes. "Don't look. You'll get nightmares."

Johnny snapped at Ben's hand.

"Oh, right," said Ben. "You *are* the nightmare."

Then Ben's gaze landed on something *truly* menacing. Halfway up the fortress, there were figures moving in a lit window. Even at a distance, he recognized them.

"Hatchet and Flip," he said. "Logan's cronies." They were dangerous, unpredictable, and cruel. The fortress wasn't the safe haven Ben had hoped for.

But it wasn't safe *outside* of the fortress, either. Ben scanned the darkness for enemies. He knew it was only a matter of time before some creature came lurching forward to attack.

"Aw, slimeballs," Ben muttered under his breath. "Any ideas, Johnny?"

The zombie boy growled unhelpfully.

Not for the first time—and not for the last—Ben wished that

Bobbie were there with them. Because at this moment, Ben was strongly considering launching an assault on two expert combatants on their home turf. He could use some backup.

Or even better: He could use someone there to talk him out of the whole thing.

CHAPTER 4

Bobbie had never been much of a risk-taker. Not so long ago, even the sight of Johnny jumping on top of a bed had been enough to make her nervous. What if he fell and hit his head? What if he broke the bed, and while shearing wool to make a new one, Bobbie accidentally hurt the village sheep?

But Bobbie's whole life had been turned upside down since the night of the zombie raid. And taking risks? That was just part of being alive!

Didn't mean she had to be *reckless*, though.

She waited to make her move until Other Ben was asleep. It was easy to tell when sleep finally took him. Other Ben didn't snore, but he did toss and turn and kick, as if trying to outrun some hostile mob that pursued him in his dreams. It was proba- bly a result of spending all his waking hours—and all his nonwaking hours, too—in such close proximity to the zombie horde. That's the sort of situation that could make a person anxious.

But Other Ben was worried about the wrong things. The zombies couldn't get to him while he slept, but *Bobbie* could. He had no idea that she was so close . . . and creeping steadily closer.

Her plan was simple. If she could steal the turtle eggs that Other Ben used to lure the zombies forward, then the horde's march would be stalled. Probably Logan would have to leave the zombies behind while he searched aboveground for new eggs. And while he did that, Bobbie could work on a more permanent solution. Maybe she'd get the horde to follow her, and she could keep them somewhere safe while she sought the golden apples that she needed to cure them.

First things first, though. She had to get those eggs away from Other Ben.

There was a sudden flash of movement in the corner of her eye. Something was descending from the ceiling—and heading past her, right toward Other Ben and the rabble of zombies beyond him.

It was a bat. Were bats hostile? Bobbie wasn't sure—but she did know that they made noise, and the last thing she needed now was for Other Ben to wake up and see her crouched in the middle of the tunnel.

She had only a split second to make her decision. Should she dash back to her hiding place? Or try to stop the bat before it could cause a commotion?

It was an easy decision. If she went back now, she'd have to wait another day before making her move. And how many more days did she have before Logan set his army loose on whatever target they were marching toward?

Bobbie acted quickly, drawing a diamond pickaxe from her inventory. A pickaxe wasn't really meant to be a weapon, but any diamond tool would make short work of a simple bat. And time was of the essence.

She leaped straight up and swung wide.

The pickaxe found its target, slashing the bat right out of the sky. That was all it took. The bat disappeared in a brief burst of dust.

She allowed herself a moment of pride. The bat hadn't exactly been a fearsome foe, but Bobbie took the encounter as evidence that her combat skills had improved. She didn't especially *like* fighting, but she had a feeling that there would be a lot more combat in her future.

Which led her to her question: How exactly should she handle Other Ben? Was taking the turtle eggs from him really enough to stop whatever Logan was planning?

She stood over the boy as he slept. He had gone to bed with his leather armor on. It looked too big on him, like it was swallowing him up. Like he was a little kid playing dress-up.

But he wasn't a little kid. He was Logan's ally. And whatever Logan was planning . . . he couldn't do it without Other Ben.

Bobbie looked from the boy's low-level armor to her high-level pickaxe. The diamond tool would pierce leather like shears through wool.

And Bobbie had to ask herself: Just how far was she willing to go to stop Logan?

CHAPTER 5

"I don't like our odds on this one, Johnny," said Ben. They were standing on a high platform just outside Fort Rot, and Ben was peering through a narrow window. The fortress was built right into the side of a mountain, made almost entirely of stone. It wasn't much to look at—Logan's builds were rarely artful—but it was well built for defense. Unless Ben wanted to dig through a solid mountain—and he didn't—his attack would have to be a direct one.

For now, their mission was simply to spy. Ben had built a little platform up against the fort's outer wall, high enough that anyone coming out of the front gate below would probably fail to notice him. And if Hatchet and Flip looked out any of the windows, they'd see the empty plateau, not the enemy clinging to the side of their fort.

"I mean, technically, our odds are two against two," Ben continued. "But those two are tough! And you're, you know . . ."

Johnny growled.

"I was going to say you're a baby, but you make a good point: You're also a *zombie*. And Flip and Hatchet are experienced zombie wranglers. They helped Logan amass his army, remember?"

Johnny groaned.

"You're right, I *am* very good at combat. But I still don't like these odds." Ben couldn't actually understand the zombie boy's guttural noises, but it made him feel better to imagine that he could. He turned to Johnny. "It's like this. Imagine I get in a fight with those two. First of all, they're better equipped — they have better armor, better weapons, and they've probably got loads of food and potions, too. Plus, consider their choice of weapons. Hatchet's got that axe of hers, and Flip has a crossbow. You can bet they know how to work as a team. If one of them gets in close, and the other is attacking from a distance, then at least one of them is going to get some hits in!

"Besides, I have you to worry about. I promised Bobbie I'd keep you safe! So a direct fight is out of the question." He sighed. "I don't like it. But I think we need to reconsider this whole idea. Maybe go back to our house on the prairie. I could rebuild it. Maybe dig a little moat or put up a fence. Bobbie would find us eventually . . . I hope . . ."

Johnny made a noise that sounded quite a bit like a complaint.

"I just don't see what other options we have."

At that moment, a door swung open, and Hatchet pushed into the room on the other side of the window. Ben ducked lower as she came into view. "I swear I heard something."

Flip followed her. "Like what? This place is empty, other than us."

"It sounded like a zombie," Hatchet answered.

"I knew it!" said Flip. "I knew Logan didn't take them all with him. There are zombies in here with us!"

"Calm down," said Hatchet. "Do you see any zombies in here?"

"Th-they could be invisible," said Flip. "They could be ghosts!"

"Don't be ridiculous," said Hatchet. "There's no such thing as ghost zombies."

"Then maybe there's zombies in the walls," said Flip. "Or in a secret passageway somewhere. This place is huge. I don't think I've even seen all of the rooms yet!"

"Well, that's true," said Hatchet. "There are all sorts of places a stray troublemaker could be hiding in here." She grunted. "We should do a sweep. Make sure the zombies are all gone. There were a lot of them, after all, and things got pretty chaotic before Logan left."

Hatchet spoke with authority, but Ben caught the note of worry in her voice.

And that was when he knew he had a chance to beat Hatchet and Flip. Not in a direct fight, of course . . .

But if they were superstitious? If they were afraid? That was knowledge Ben could use against them.

And maybe, for once . . . Johnny would be a help.

Ben searched his inventory. As luck would have it, he had everything he needed to make a fermented spider eye. And the golden carrot would come in handy, too.

As Ben began removing his armor, Johnny looked at him quizzically.

"Trust me," Ben said. "I've got a plan."

Johnny, it had to be said, did not look entirely reassured.

CHAPTER 6

"Hey, kid," Bobbie said, low and urgent. "Wake up!"

She shook him for good measure. But very lightly! She didn't want to freak him out *too* much.

Other Ben's eyes flew open. That was good. He was awake!

But his mouth opened, too. That could be bad. Bobbie quickly covered his mouth with her free hand.

"Shh!" she said. "Don't make a sound!"

She meant it as more of a polite request than a threat. But Other Ben's eyes shifted to the diamond pickaxe in her other hand, and she saw he was afraid.

Bobbie probably should have anticipated that. After all, she'd pulled the sleeping boy from his bed, dragged him across the tunnel, and shoved him into the dark, claustrophobic hiding spot she'd carved into the stone and dirt.

Other Ben was a *very* heavy sleeper.

"D-don't hurt me!" he said.

"I'm not going to hurt you," Bobbie whispered, and she put away the pickaxe. "I'm the good guy, remember? Now keep your voice down."

Other Ben took in his new surroundings. "You kidnapped me!" he said. "Do good guys kidnap people?"

Bobbie rolled her eyes. "I hardly kidnapped you. We're like ten steps away from your camp. Look, I just wanted to talk, okay? And I thought we'd better do it away from the murder horde."

"And away from Logan, right?" said Other Ben. "He wouldn't be happy to find you here." Other Ben lowered his voice, as if finally realizing the risk Bobbie was taking. "He's a great fighter, and he's got a grudge against you. If he finds you here, he'll *destroy* you."

"He'll try," Bobbie said, striking a pose that—she hoped— made her look confident and competent. "He's tried more than once, and I'm still here."

"I guess," said Other Ben.

Bobbie continued, "You don't have to worry about Logan hurting me. But I'll confess that I'm worried what'll happen when he turns on *you*."

"He . . . he wouldn't do that," Other Ben said slowly. "He's my friend."

Bobbie gave him a skeptical look.

"Okay, well, maybe not my friend, but he's my mentor. He's training me! So that one day I'll be as skilled as he is."

"From what I've seen, Logan's skills amount to getting other people to do his dirty work . . . and taking easy shots at zombies from a safe distance. I think you should aim a little higher, young Benjamin. And what's with this armor?" Bobbie tugged on his helmet, and it fell over his eyes. "He's got you in his over-size hand-me-downs while he gets a full set of diamond duds? When *you're* the one who has to be zombie bait all day? How is that fair?"

"I've got to earn my way," Other Ben said, clearly reciting words that Logan had drilled into him. He righted his helmet. "And I'd definitely earn a lot of points by telling him *you're* here!"

"I don't think you'll do that, though," Bobbie said, giving him a serious look. "I think you're a good kid, and I don't think you want to see Logan *destroy* me or anybody else. The way he tried to destroy his last Ben buddy."

Other Ben huffed. "That guy was annoying! Sorry, I know he's your friend—"

"No, you're right," Bobbie conceded. "On both counts. He's my friend, but he's also super annoying."

"Well, he messed up too many times, and Logan cut him loose." Other Ben crossed his arms. "But that's not going to happen to me."

"I hope you're right," said Bobbie. "But you should ask yourself what kind of person cuts a friend loose by taking all his stuff and abandoning him in the night."

Other Ben frowned. "Just stay out of our way," he said, and he turned to go. "You don't know anything about either of us. I'm loyal to Logan. Don't test me."

Other Ben stomped off, his too-big helmet sliding around

with each step. Bobbie didn't call after him, and she didn't try to stop him. Nor did she try to take the turtle eggs. She had a new plan, a better plan, and she figured it was going exactly as intended.

She had planted just the smallest seed of doubt in Other Ben's mind. Given time, that seed would grow.

And down here, on the march?

Down here, they had nothing but time.

CHAPTER 7

en waited until Hatchet and Flip were sleeping. Then he went to work, as quietly as possible, on an unusual sort of construction project.

He started by building a walkway along the exterior of Fort Rot, above the second-story windows and below the ones on the third story. The walkway was narrow, just two blocks wide, and he extended it all around the fortress. He then enclosed the walkway, so that he'd built a hallway of sorts, one with no doors or windows, built right up against the outer wall of the fortress. It was perfectly symmetrical and made of the same stone as the fortress itself, which was in abundant supply in the surrounding mountain. If you hadn't known to look for it, you'd never have known it was there.

He left Johnny there, enclosed in the narrow hallway. As Ben prepared to place the last stone, Johnny looked out at him through the empty space. The zombie boy's head was tilted quizzically.

"I'll come back for you," Ben whispered. "For now, I need you where they can hear you . . . but can't *see* you." Then he placed the final block of stone, sealing Johnny away.

The next part of his plan was even trickier. It required the utmost stealth and caution. Ben built his way to the very top of the fortress, then entered through the rooftop, tiptoeing as he went.

He hoped he remembered where to find the brewing stand.

Ben watched as Flip awoke with a start. The boy had heard something—a sound that didn't belong in the safety of the fortress. Or had he only dreamed it? Ben recognized the groggy confusion on Flip's features.

But Flip had no idea that Ben was in the room, watching.

"Hatchet," Flip said urgently. "Did you hear that?"

"Muh whu?" said Hatchet, slower to wake.

A low growl sounded.

"That!" said Flip. "You heard that, right?"

"It's just a zombie," Hatchet said, turning over in her bed.

"Just a zombie!" Flip echoed. "That sound is definitely coming from inside the fortress!"

"There *are* no zombies inside the fortress," said Hatchet. "We looked everywhere. It's probably outside," she added.

"But it's daytime!" argued Flip.

Hatchet sighed, finally giving up on going back to sleep. She planted her heavy feet on the ground—she had slept in her armor, boots and all—and she cast a murderous look in Flip's direction. "I'm sure there's a perfectly reasonable explanation," she said.

But when another growl sounded, Hatchet jumped out of bed, alarmed. She spun in a circle. "Okay, that sounded like it was *right* behind me."

"That's what I've been saying," said Flip.

"But there's nothing there."

"That's what I've been saying!" said Flip.

And then, suddenly, a torch fell from the wall.

Hatchet and Flip both shrieked in surprise.

It took everything Ben had not to laugh.

Being invisible sure had its perks.

Hatchet and Flip ran from their bedroom and into the hallway. Ben followed, invisible to their eyes and as silent as he could be. Fortunately, Johnny—left alone in the completely enclosed hallway—chose that moment to make more noise.

"Grawr!"

"It's a zombie!" said Flip.

Ben knocked down another torch, and another. The light in the hallway dimmed.

"It's a ghost!" said Hatchet.

They stepped away from the falling torches . . . and right onto a pressure plate that Ben had hidden in the floor while they'd slept. All the hallway's many doors slammed open at the same moment.

"It's zombie ghosts!" cried Flip. "A whole horde of them!"

"Run!" shouted Hatchet, and as they fled down the hallway, Ben followed, knocking down torches and hitting a series of pressure plates so that the doors all shut and then opened and then shut once again.

His Potion of Invisibility expired just as the pair bolted out Fort Rot's open front gate. But that was perfect timing.

Hatchet and Flip kept running, not daring to look back.

And Ben finally allowed himself to laugh.

CHAPTER 8

The day after Bobbie's confrontation with Other Ben started out like any other day. Bobbie watched from the shadows as Other Ben packed up his things and then hurried to meet Logan at the front of the horde. She thought he might look back in the direction of her hiding spot, but he didn't spare her a glance. To be fair, he needed to keep both eyes on the zombies as he removed the fencing in order to stay out of their clawing grasp. It was a highly hazardous job.

The rest of the day was a slow, trudging march, with Bobbie hanging back, just out of range of the back row of zombies. But when Logan sounded the goat horn, calling for a stop to the march, Bobbie was certain it wasn't night yet. Why had they traveled such a short distance?

She hated to think it, but what if she'd been wrong about

Other Ben? What if he'd sold her out to Logan? She'd have no choice but to fight.

But while Logan was spoiling for a fight, it wasn't with her.

"What are you doing?" hissed Other Ben as he reappeared at the back of the horde, replacing the fencing he'd just taken down a little while ago. "Why are you still following us?"

"Because I've got a sneaking suspicion you're up to no good," Bobbie answered. "The hundreds of zombies were my first clue."

Other Ben bit his lip as he placed another piece of fence. He appeared to be debating whether or not to tell her something.

"What is it?" Bobbie asked. "Why did we stop?"

"None of your business," said Other Ben. "Stop following us! And stop trying to turn me against Logan." He put the last piece of fence down more forcefully than necessary. "He's my friend! You're not!"

At that, he stomped away, heading around the fence toward the front of the horde.

And that's when Bobbie noticed a beam of sunlight in the tunnel up ahead. It was a narrow shaft shining down from above, as if someone had cut a single block out of the tunnel's high ceiling.

Logan had gone aboveground.

Bobbie knew she had to follow.

Breathing fresh air for the first time in days—feeling the sunlight on her skin—Bobbie felt her spirits lift despite the urgency of her mission.

The tunnel she'd been walking, she knew, had taken them under the ocean that bordered Logan's fortress. She had walked to a completely different continent, right under the sea!

She emerged in a jungle, packed thick with towering trees strung with vines. She heard whistling and squawking from above. A parrot? She'd never seen one before! She scanned the canopy, then hopped up a steep ridge to get a better view.

The view was more interesting than she'd anticipated. In the middle distance, across a high plateau, was a tower. It was impressively tall, made of wood and stone, and its slanted rooftop almost appeared to be stretching for the sun. She could see figures moving along its various levels.

They were people. Villagers!

Bobbie could hardly believe her luck. Villagers meant supplies, maybe even help against Logan—or at the very least, a sympathetic ear. After so long on her own, Bobbie craved the company of other people.

She'd never heard of a vertical village before, but she'd seen a lot of strange things since leaving Plaintown. It only made sense that the strangeness would be more pronounced here, on an entirely different continent.

She ran across the plateau as fast as her feet would take her. "Hello!" she cried, waving her arms. "Hi, there!"

A sound of alarm went up as soon as the figures became aware of her presence. Within seconds, an arrow flew toward her, embedding itself in the dirt at her feet.

Bobbie stopped in her tracks. She took a big step back and put her hands up. She'd lived with villagers all her life, and she'd never seen one do anything aggressive. Even when zombies had attacked her village, the people there hadn't shot arrows; they'd fled. Could these villagers really be so different?

"There's no need for hostility," she shouted up at the tower. "I come in peace!"

Several more arrows flew through the air, and Bobbie turned and ran back the way she'd come.

"Why does everyone want to fight *all the time*?" she cried. "Doesn't anyone ever just want to sit down with a bowl of soup and *talk*?"

An arrow, whizzing past her head, was the only answer she received. Judging by the angle it traveled, it had been shot from ground level. One of the tower-dwellers was following her!

Bobbie jumped behind a tree trunk and drew her sword. She could hear her pursuer drawing near. "Fine, you want to fight?" she said. "We'll fight."

Bobbie stepped out from behind the tree, holding her sword high. Her attacker looked like an average villager, but with gray skin and sleek leather armor. On their back, hoisted high above their head, the figure wore a banner with a scowling face. She'd heard stories of people like this—not villagers, but *pillagers*, known for their aggression . . . and their vicious crossbows.

Bobbie felt a moment of doubt. Could she prevail in a battle against a pillager?

She was about to find out.

CHAPTER 9

Ben found that he quite enjoyed having an entire fortress all to himself.

Well, *almost* all to himself. He'd let Johnny out of the hallway enclosure by breaking through a second-story wall as soon as Hatchet and Flip had fled. Now Johnny had the run of the fortress, too. The zombie boy still wore his lead, but Ben decided not to tie him to a post. The place was locked up tight, so Johnny couldn't wander too far.

Logan had emptied a lot of his loot chests before leaving. But a person could carry only so much, and so Logan had left behind more than a few useful items. Ben found a few armor upgrades—used items that he was able to cobble into better shape on the courtyard anvil. There were plentiful potions, and fresh milk, and choice cuts of meat, which he cooked in one of the many furnaces lining the dining hall. He even found a pristine white bone for Johnny to gnaw on! (He didn't care to wonder where the bone had come from.) There were a few odd touches, such as a charged creeper head in a trophy room. The courtyard's turtle pen had been emptied of turtles, although some scute had been left behind, and for some reason the pigpen had what looked like some kind of iron fence. Those small oddities aside, the fortress was a tremendous improvement over Ben's previous circumstances.

And the bedroom! Since becoming an adventurer, Ben had been constantly on the move, rarely staying in the same place for more than a night or two, building temporary shelters out of whatever pieces of debris he could dig up. His most recent semi-permanent shelter, the one he'd lost to a creeper, had left a lot to be desired. By contrast, Logan's abandoned bedroom was the height of luxury, with paintings on the walls, lanterns instead of torches, and a soft bed dyed a peaceful shade of blue. Ben made himself comfortable. It was an easy thing to do.

One particular painting sort of creeped him out, however. It was dominated by the image of a skull. He turned away from it, but he couldn't shake the feeling that the skull was looking at him. Comfortable bed or not, he'd never be able to get to sleep with skeletal eye sockets pointing right at him.

He groaned, lifting himself from bed and crossing the room, then he unceremoniously slapped the painting off the wall.

To his surprise, there was a hidden compartment behind the painting—a gap in the otherwise uniform stonework. But there weren't any riches or rare weapons stashed away. The only thing in the compartment . . . was a book.

That was unusual, to say the least. The boys had spent a lot of time together, and Ben knew very well that Logan wasn't much of a reader. And he certainly wasn't the type of person to treat a book as if it were a precious treasure. What sort of book was this, exactly? Ben cracked the cover to take a look.

The pages within were filled with handwriting. Logan's handwriting.

Ben quickly slammed the book shut.

It was obvious what this was. Logan . . . had kept a *journal*. This was news to Ben. Either it was a new hobby that Logan had taken up since they'd parted ways, or else Logan had been very careful to keep the journal from Ben's view. The latter possibility hinted at secrecy bordering on paranoia . . . but Ben had already accepted that he'd never really known Logan. Not truly.

He reached again for the journal. Hesitated. It would be *wrong* to read it. Right? It would be.

Just then, a shadow fell over Ben. "Aah!" he shrieked, spinning around. "I wasn't doing anything wrong!"

Johnny stood in the doorway with a blank expression on his face. Clearly, the young zombie wasn't judging Ben for being a snoop.

The guilt Ben felt was coming entirely from within himself.

"This is me being a good role model," Ben said, and he replaced the creepy painting, leaving the book where he'd found it. "Just remember this if you're ever tempted to read your sister's journal. They're private!"

Johnny emitted a rasping breath. The boy had seemed listless all day, wandering from room to room as if looking for something. Ben wondered: How much did Johnny remember? Did he realize this was the last place that he and Ben had seen Bobbie? Did he expect to find her here?

"Come on," said Ben. "Come with me. I want to show you something."

He led Johnny to the center of the fortress, to the now empty chamber where Logan had kept his countless zombies penned. Ben looked up at the balcony from which Logan had kept an eye on the horde; he could almost imagine his old friend looking down at him in disapproval, eager for the entertainment of watching Ben battle—and succumb to—a crushing wave of the undead.

Ben shook it off, bringing his eyes back to ground level. He was standing in the very spot Bobbie had stood when she'd sent them racing down a tunnel to safety. But where had she gone from there?

There were several tunnels leading off the central chamber. They'd all been blocked off. Ben recognized the tunnel he and Johnny had traveled through, but Logan and Bobbie might have taken any of the other tunnels. There was no way to know for certain which direction to take . . . and choosing poorly could mean that Bobbie would be lost to them forever.

Ben hoped to see his friend again. And he certainly hoped to return her zombified brother to her care. Raising a zombie was a lot of work!

"She'll come back," said Ben. "One day, she'll bust through one of these walls and tell us all about her adventures. And I'll bet she'll have a cure for you, too," he said, patting Johnny's head. "But in the meantime, you and I are going to stay here, where it's safe, where the beds are soft, and where we have all the food we can eat."

Johnny growled, and it sounded like disagreement.

"I'm sorry, but that's final!" said Ben. "What would you suggest? That we pick a tunnel at random? Get hopelessly lost? We don't know what Logan was planning, and we don't have any way to find out!"

Johnny gnawed on his bone and blinked. His beady little eyes seemed to gaze into Ben's soul . . . and call him rude names.

Ben realized his mistake. He did have one way to learn more about Logan's plans.

"Oh, man," he said, remembering that eerie skull painting and what it hid. "I'm totally going to have to read Logan's journal, aren't I?"

He had a feeling it wouldn't have nice things to say about him.

CHAPTER 10

Bobbie gripped her sword. The pillager was drawing near—and drawing back the string of their crossbow. At this range, their next arrow wouldn't miss.

All in a rush, Ben's combat lessons came back to Bobbie. When armed with a sword and fighting a ranged foe, the trick was to close the distance. She would have to rush forward and quickly close the gap. It was her only hope of winning this fight. She took a single step forward—

Suddenly, an explosion rang out. An explosion . . . and unhinged laughter. Both had come from the direction of the pillager outpost.

Bobbie's foe turned toward the sounds of chaos. Seemingly forgetting all about Bobbie, they ran for the outpost, and, keeping her distance, Bobbie followed.

In the short time since Bobbie had last seen it, the outpost had descended into chaos. A smoldering hole had been blasted into the stony base of the tower. Bobbie suspected TNT had been set off, and, judging by the arrows littering the ground, several pillagers had been caught in the blast.

But TNT didn't just blow up on its own. And Bobbie quickly discovered the culprit: Logan was there, wading into the chaos, his diamond sword raised high and his shield held out before him. Two pillagers rushed to meet him, their crossbows raised— but they never had a chance to fire a single shot. Logan careened between them, a glittering blue blur of violence. He hacked and slashed, he darted and jumped, and in the time it took Bobbie to gasp, he felled both of his opponents. He made it look effortless.

Other Ben had been right. Logan had skills.

But Bobbie was less surprised to see that Logan's skills did not include a talent for taking care of others. Other Ben was there, in his hand-me-down armor and sad stone sword, running in a hapless zigzag pattern to avoid the arrows raining down from above. Logan didn't even seem to notice. Instead of doubling back to help his squire, he forged ahead, taking the first of many staircases up the tower.

The pillager that had previously come after Bobbie now had its sights set on Other Ben. As Bobbie watched, it raised its crossbow, preparing to fire at its unsuspecting victim.

But two could play at that game. Bobbie charged into action, catching the pillager off guard. She slashed with her sword, putting all her strength behind the swing.

It wasn't enough to defeat the pillager, though it certainly got the mob's attention. The pillager whirled on Bobbie, and Bobbie reeled back in surprise, stumbling over her own two feet. The pillager fired off a shot with their crossbow, but as Bobbie tumbled backward, the arrow sailed harmlessly over her head.

"Ha!" she said. "I meant to do that."

Bobbie took advantage of her low position—and the crossbow's reload time—and slashed out twice with her sword, cutting her foe across their ankles. Crouching low to the ground, she hurried to get behind the pillager, who fired a series of arrows into the dirt as they spun in a circle, trying to get a bead on Bobbie. She stabbed them in the foot.

When the pillager finally fell, they left no trace except for a fallen crossbow.

It wasn't a dignified victory. But it was a victory. Bobbie would take it. (And she took the crossbow, too.)

She looked back to the outpost. The assault was in full swing now, and Logan had fought his way halfway up the tower. Other Ben was trailing a floor behind him. At the moment, he was in a standoff with another pillager—and it wasn't going well for the young squire. The pillager was hopping lightly on its feet, staying just beyond the reach of Other Ben's sword and firing arrows into the boy every time he took another futile swing.

How much more could Other Ben take? Would Logan notice in time to come to the boy's aid?

Bobbie couldn't wait around to find out. She aimed her newly acquired crossbow and fired an arrow at Other Ben's adversary. It struck the pillager right in the back, knocking the mob forward . . . into the range of Other Ben's sword.

As Other Ben finally connected, slashing the pillager into oblivion, he looked up. Even at a distance, he saw Bobbie immediately. Their eyes locked, and for a moment, she worried that he would call out to Logan. Bobbie knew now that she had no hope of taking Logan in a fight.

But Other Ben didn't call out. He held Bobbie's eyes for a moment, and then he nodded, somberly, in thanks. Then he turned to follow Logan into the final battle with the remaining pillagers.

It was then that a thought occurred to Bobbie. She had hit that pillager with an arrow from this distance.

What was keeping her from doing the same to Logan? If she timed it right, she could knock him clear off the tower!

She held up the crossbow and scanned the structure for Logan. He was using a shield to deflect a pillager's attack, so he'd be occupied for at least a little while longer. Long enough for Bobbie to line up her shot and let her arrow fly. And why shouldn't she do it? With Logan out of the picture, the zombies would stay put right where they were, penned up in an underground tunnel, until Bobbie could track down enough golden apples to cure every last one of them. She would no longer have to worry about what Logan had in store for them. She could find Ben, and Johnny, and together they could fix everything.

All it would take was a sneak attack on the vengeful, selfish, coldhearted boy who had set this whole nightmare into motion. One well-placed arrow, and everything could go back to normal.

But she couldn't do it.

It was too callous. Too cruel. Fighting in self-defense was one thing. But she'd never be able to look Johnny in the eye if she hurt someone else just to make her life a little easier.

She stashed the crossbow in her inventory. The fight, for her, was over.

She noticed that she was standing beneath an apple tree, and she realized that she was hungry. She took a piece of fruit, and just as she was about to bite into it, a nearby flash of color caught her eye.

There were cages near the base of the tower. Prisons, Bobbie suspected. They were all empty, except for one, which held a small blue creature, so small that Bobbie had almost looked right past it.

She crept closer for a better look. The creature was unlike anything she'd seen before, with busy blue wings and big white eyes. It was cute—something between an insect and a ghost. It reminded her a little bit of the vex she'd seen at a woodland mansion, but this creature was smaller and much less frightening.

It also apparently couldn't travel through walls like a vex could. The creature pushed against the bars of its cage, to no avail.

Bobbie decided to let it out. *Whatever* it was, it didn't deserve to be locked up, and it certainly didn't deserve to end up in Logan's clutches.

Bobbie crept forward, hoping that the final pillager—or its loot—would keep Other Ben and Logan occupied just a little bit longer. She crouched as she approached the cage, and as soon as she was in range, she smashed it open with her pickaxe.

The creature made no immediate move to flee. It turned its big white eyes on Bobbie and cooed.

"Are you hungry?" Bobbie whispered. She realized she was still holding the freshly picked apple in her off hand, and she held it out to the mob. "Here. Take it."

The creature accepted the apple graciously. It giggled, making an almost tinkling sound, then flew off.

Bobbie was a little jealous. There was a part of her that would sincerely have liked to fly away from this place—away from Logan and pillagers and subterranean zombie hordes lurking just out of sight—and never look back.

But she still had a job to do. People were depending on her.

So she found a new hiding spot, close enough to keep an eye on Logan.

She had a perfect view of his victory over the final pillager. The outcome of the battle was clear.

This outpost belonged to Logan.

CHAPTER 11

Ben was alone, and he was afraid.

By the light of day, the thought of a solo adventure—just him against the elements!—had been so exciting.

Now, by the cold light of the moon, Ben realized his mistake. He didn't know the first thing about adventuring. It had taken him all morning to gather enough wood to begin crafting basic tools. Carving stone with his wooden pickaxe had been painfully slow, and he hadn't found nearly enough coal to make as many torches as he wanted.

And the sun had gone down so *quickly*.

Now Ben was hiding in his first-ever shelter—which was actually more of a *hole* than a shelter, just a narrow space he'd cut out of a hill. He had managed to craft a simple wooden door—he was proud of that—but a bed had been too complicated, so as much as he would have liked to have curled up and slept through the night, he had no choice but to stand there in his sad stone hallway, waiting for the night to pass.

Ben shuddered. He heard the telltale groan of a zombie coming from just outside his little shelter. The sound was strangely familiar to Ben. Something gnawed at his mind. Where was he? *When* was he?

This was all a dream, wasn't it?

Not just a dream, he realized. A *memory*. An important one.

Ben remembered very clearly what had happened next.

Anxious and impatient, Ben had decided to dig. He wanted more coal, and iron for weapons, and maybe even redstone, although he wouldn't have known what to do with it if he found it. More than all that, he wanted to have something to do with his hands. If he just stood here all night long, staring at his torch and listening to the monsters outside, there was a very real chance that he would have a panic attack, run all the way to the nearest village, and hide in a library attic for the rest of his life.

So he dug.

Things went wrong almost immediately.

Ben's wooden pickaxe broke through stone, and instead of revealing *more* stone, it revealed a dark, empty space. There was a *cavern* on the other side of Ben's narrow shelter. He leaned forward for a better look . . .

And he got a face full of bat.

Ben panicked, and the bat panicked, too. They both screamed—the bat was higher pitched, but only by a little. As it flapped around the small, enclosed space, Ben tried to slap it out of the air, but it was too fast, its flying too frantic. As its wings slapped across his vision, he leaped backward, pushing through the door and out into the night.

Once outside, he quickly ran afoul of an enderman. The creature shrieked, lashing out at Ben with its inhumanly long arms. Ben was armed with only a half-broken wooden pickaxe, and he wasn't able to land a single strike with it. Every time he swung for the mob, it teleported away, reappearing at Ben's back and renewing its attack.

Ben fell to his knees. He closed his eyes, waiting for the enderman to deliver the killing blow.

But the mob never got a chance. There was the sound of an iron sword singing on the wind, and triumphant laughter. Ben opened his eyes just in time to see the mob fall over, defeated. A boy bent over to pick up the inky pearl it had left behind.

"Uh, h-hello?" said Ben.

The boy looked at him then. He flashed a crooked smile. "Hey. You didn't look at the enderman, did you? They hate that." He extended a hand. "I'm Logan."

Ben smiled. For the first time since the moon had risen, he felt safe.

Thunder echoed through the bedchamber, and Ben jolted awake. The lanterns were still lit. He had dozed off while reading Logan's journal.

Although, in truth, it was more of a burn book than a journal.

Ben turned to reread Logan's account of their first meeting—the night that had left such a lasting impression on Ben and shaped his career as an adventurer. Logan's entry read:

"Saved some idiot's butt today. Now he's following me around like a tame wolf."

Yep, thought Ben. It hurt just as much to read that the second time as it had the first time.

As guilty as Ben felt for violating someone's privacy this way, he had at least thought he might gain some true insight into who Logan was as a person. Where had he grown up? Had he always wanted to be an adventurer?

Had he ever actually enjoyed Ben's company, even a little?

But Logan hadn't written much. He hadn't poured his heart out in flowery paragraphs, as Ben had imagined. Instead he'd jotted down insults, kept lists, drawn diagrams, and made little doodles.

The lists were mostly things that Logan disliked: "5 Worst Biomes Ever." "Most Useless Enchantments." "Top 5 Annoying Mobs." (Ben was horrified to find axolotls on the top of the list—seriously, who hated axolotls?! Meanwhile, llamas, which were objectively the worst animal, had been left off the list entirely.)

There was one page titled "Number of times Ben messed something up." The tally there was way too high. Ben assumed it must be about Other Ben. (It *must* be!)

Thunder rumbled just outside the window, and Ben doubted he'd get back to sleep anytime soon. He kept flipping through the pages. There were diagrams for zombie traps, like the one Ben and Bobbie had fallen into the first time they'd approached the fortress, and for the "iron farm" Logan had built to force villagers to produce endless supplies of iron ingots. There was even a diagram for harnessing lightning to transform cute little pigs into zombified piglins. Ben shuddered at the illustration of a two-legged, dead-eyed pig beast and hoped that particular diagram was pure fantasy. Who would want to create an undead pig monster?

Ben had history with zombified piglins. It wasn't a *good* history.

Interestingly, near the back of the book, there was a "To-Do" list written in Logan's sloppy handwriting. Ben sat up in bed and leaned in close. He read:

Recruit grunts for labor: [x]

Dig tunnels: [x]

Amass zombie army: [x]

Cross the sea and take over an outpost: [ ]

Outfit the army: [ ]

Overthrow the Overworld Overlords: [ ]

Pulverize Pigstep Peggy: [ ]

Ben's jaw dropped open. He didn't know any Peggys, but he'd heard a lot of stories about the Overworld Overlords. Every adventurer knew the Overlords, and every adventurer—Ben included—dreamed of joining their ranks one day. They were the best of the best. The most fearsome fighters, the most meticulous miners, the craftiest crafters . . .

And now they were in Logan's crosshairs. And with an army of the undead at his command, Logan just might succeed in destroying them.

Ben couldn't let that happen. He had to warn the Overlords. Ben looked at the page again and realized that Logan had written *coordinates* beside that item on his to-do list. It had to be where the Overlords had built their famous headquarters. It was supposed to be the size of a village!

Lightning flashed outside, and a thunderclap shook the fortress. Ben shuddered, remembering Logan's illustration of the pig creature.

And then Ben remembered something else he had seen.

He stuck his head out the window, for a view of the courtyard below. There was the pigpen, and what Ben had thought was a strange use of metal in the construction of its fence . . . was something else entirely.

It was a lightning rod. Several of them, in fact.

Oh no, thought Ben. Was Logan trying to *create* one of those creatures in his own courtyard?!

Ben bolted from the room. He passed Johnny, who was wandering the hallway idly and turned to watch Ben as he passed.

"Minor emergency!" Ben called over his shoulder. "You're not ready for a monstrous sibling, right? I know I'm not ready!"

He hurried downstairs and flung open the inner door to the courtyard. The rain was coming down, and lightning flashed frequently in the clouds above. He would have to act quickly.

Logan had set multiple lightning rods all around the perimeter of the pigpen. Ben would have to grab all of them, to be safe.

He picked up the first one. The pig looked up at him and oinked, as if to ask what he was up to.

"I'm doing this for your own good!" Ben said. "Well, yours *and* mine . . ."

Ben reached through a curtain of rain, intending to grab a second lightning rod. He almost had it—

And then a bolt of lightning seared the air in front of him. It looked as if the world itself were splitting open.

Ben was blown off his feet. He didn't even realize it had happened until he noticed his hands were in the mud. His vision was white, but as he blinked, the brightness faded, giving way to indistinct, shadowy forms. He blinked harder and saw one of those shadows coalesce into a looming figure. It reached out its hand, as if to aid him.

"L-Logan?" Ben said. "Or . . . or Bobbie, is th-that you?"

And then the figure took a lumbering step forward, and Ben knew it was not his friend.

It stood on two legs, but it was decidedly inhuman, with the prominent snout, pink skin, and floppy ears of a pig. But its flesh was rotting away in sickly green streaks, and where the flesh had fallen off completely, white bone showed through. Fully half its face was a fleshless skull, and several sharp ribs poked through the broken skin of its chest.

It was a zombified piglin. Ben hadn't seen one in ages. And it was every bit as unnerving as he remembered—far more gruesome than an average zombie.

Ben shrieked in horror. He tried to regain his footing, but his legs wouldn't respond. He couldn't do anything but scrabble backward, dragging himself across the muddy ground with his arms, while he shrieked himself raw.

The zombie pig-person was armed with a gleaming sword, and it took another shambling step forward, fixing Ben with its eerie eyes—one white and wet, one an empty black socket in a bone-white skull. Ben froze beneath its uncanny gaze.

But the creature did not attack. It snorted, tilted its head as if confused by Ben's terrified noises, and then it shuffled off, entering the fortress through the door Ben had left open.

"Rawr?" said a voice from behind Ben, and he shrieked once more, even as he realized that Johnny was there, standing in the rain, giving him the same confused look that the pig-beast had given him.

"We're leaving!" said Ben. "We're leaving right now. Come on!" He grabbed the lead and started running in a random direction. There was no wrong direction, he decided, so long as they didn't stay *here*.

Johnny, whether pleased with the development or just naturally agreeable, came along without complaint.

CHAPTER 12

The flying blue mob found Bobbie's hiding spot easily.

It flew right up to her and cooed, handing Bobbie an apple. Apparently, it wanted to repay her.

"Aw, thanks," she whispered. "But can you fly a little lower? You're going to give me away . . ."

Bobbie was crouching behind a shrub, and she'd put down a few blocks of dirt for good measure. She was as close to the pillager outpost—*Logan's* outpost now—as she dared to get. She hoped it was close enough to eavesdrop on Logan's scheming.

Lucky for her, Logan spoke loudly—and *often*. The boy seemed to love the sound of his own voice.

"This place is perfect!" said Logan. "Did you go to the top? You can see for miles in every direction!"

NICK ELIOPULOS

"It made me feel a little dizzy," said Other Ben. "And *small*. The Overworld is so big."

Bobbie nodded to herself. She'd felt the exact same way her first time looking out from a mountaintop.

"It makes me feel big," said Logan. "Like the master of all I can see. Like the king of the Overworld!" He laughed. "Anyway, you should get this place fortified. We'll be able to see any trouble coming our way, but it'd be nice if we could also, like, launch TNT at it."

"I could . . . try to figure out how to do that. What if—"

But Logan wasn't listening. "Hey! I thought there was an allay in this cage," he said, and Bobbie risked a quick peek over the dirt blocks. Logan and Other Ben were standing in front of the cage where Bobbie had found her little blue friend. An allay—was that what it was?

"The cage must have been damaged in the battle," said Other Ben. "And the allay flew off."

Bobbie saw that Other Ben was looking in her direction. She ducked back down and pulled the allay lower, too. Maybe she wasn't as sneaky as she thought.

"Oh, well," said Logan. "There will be other allays. Once our army is fully equipped—and once my enemies are overrun— this whole area will be defenseless. We'll take whatever we want, and there won't be anyone to stand in our way ever again."

"We'll see about that. Won't we, Layla?" whispered Bobbie.

The creature chirped in agreement.

———

With Logan and Other Ben taking the outpost as a new base, Bobbie had the opportunity she'd been waiting for: time alone with the zombie horde.

That wasn't something she'd have wished for a few weeks ago. Her priorities had changed pretty quickly! But as she scanned the faces of the horde, she remembered all over again that these weren't just any zombies—not all of them, at least. Mixed in with the run-of-the-mill mindless mobs were familiar faces. She saw her town cleric and farmer, the librarian and blacksmith she'd known since she was a baby. And somewhere in the crowd, she knew, were her parents.

Bobbie didn't know where she came from originally—as Ben liked to remind her, she wasn't a typical villager—but she'd been raised by villagers, and after a happy childhood full of love and support, Bobbie considered the couple who raised her to be her parents, plain and simple. She would do whatever it took to save them.

But time was of the essence. Logan might return at any moment. And Bobbie still didn't have a single dose of the cure—a combination of golden apple and Potion of Weakness. Looking at the mass of undead mobs on the far side of Other Ben's fence, Bobbie knew she'd need a lot more than a single dose.

"We've got to get these zombies away from Logan," she said, and the allay chirped and handed her an apple.

Bobbie fought the urge to roll her eyes. "Thanks. But honestly, I don't need any more—and there she goes." Bobbie sighed. Layla seemed to have a one-track mind. And in the absence of the allay's glowing aura, Bobbie's surroundings felt extra creepy. The creature gave off a subtle blue light, which was not enough to see by—Bobbie relied on the torches that Logan and Other Ben had left behind for that. But any light in this subterranean darkness was welcome, and the blue hue cast by Layla felt especially comforting.

As the nearest zombies strained against their fence enclosure, reaching for Bobbie and gnashing their teeth, Bobbie knew she would take any comfort she could get.

"Okay, okay," Bobbie said aloud to herself. "So what am I going to do with you all?"

The zombies made no reply except to rasp and groan and slash at the air.

"I could lead you off somewhere," said Bobbie. "March you right back where we came from. But without any turtle eggs, I would be the only bait. What happens when I need to stop for food or rest? What happens if some of you in the back start wandering off because I'm too far ahead?"

Bobbie sighed. She saw now why keeping this horde on the march was a two-person job. If only she hadn't sent Ben away . . .

She racked her brain for a plan. If she couldn't lead the horde away from Logan . . . could she hide them somehow? What if she dug a pit, right beneath their feet, and then covered it up again? Logan would come back to find the pen empty. If Bobbie broke a piece of fence away, he'd assume the zombies had all fled. He'd wander the tunnels looking for them, not realizing they were safe just beneath his feet.

Bobbie, meanwhile, would have all the time she needed to

gather cures. And she'd be the only one who knew where the horde was hidden. As long as she didn't get lost . . .

This plan could work. She felt it in her bones. It was a *good* plan.

She turned to the zombies. "You guys don't mind being buried in the dark for a little while, right?" she asked. "I bet you'll feel right at home!"

"It's you that's gonna be buried," said a voice, and Bobbie whirled around. She could see only a short distance up and down the torchlit tunnel.

"Who's there?" she asked.

Two figures emerged from the shadows.

"Don't tell me you forgot us?" said Hatchet, hefting her axe.

"Because we sure didn't forget you," said Flip, aiming his crossbow. "And neither did the boss, I bet. You caused Logan an awful lot of trouble back at Fort Rot."

"And he's gonna welcome us back with open arms when we tell him we got rid of you," said Hatchet. "*Permanently.*"

CHAPTER 13

Ben was pleased with the boat he had crafted. It wasn't spacious by any means. But it was big enough for both of them, and it allowed him to keep an eye on Johnny while rowing. He always felt better having the zombie boy where he could see him.

Especially when Johnny was wearing his little helmet.

"I don't care what you say," said Ben. "I think it's adorable."

The sun was high overhead, and the ocean was all around them. There was no shelter to be seen. Not even so much as a bit of shade. So Ben had had no choice but to drop the carved pumpkin over Johnny's head.

Johnny grumbled, and the sound echoed a bit within the pumpkin.

"Adorable," repeated Ben, and he looked down at his map.

They still had a long way to travel, but armed with the coordinates of the Overlords' HQ, they at least had a destination in mind. And taking the direct route—over the sea instead of *under* it—Ben hoped he'd beat Logan to the Overlords. If he was really lucky, he would catch up to Bobbie, too. After all, she was dogging Logan's steps . . . and Ben now knew where those steps were headed.

He didn't mention that part to Johnny, though. He didn't want to get the boy's hopes up. Bobbie was smart and resourceful, and she *probably* hadn't fallen into a pit of lava or been blown to bits by a creeper, but who could say for sure? The Overworld was a dangerous place, and Bobbie, as smart as she was, was still a rookie. Unlike Ben himself, who— "Ooh, dolphin!"

"Mrowr?" said Johnny.

"A dolphin! See? It's following us. And where there's one dolphin . . ."

Ben spun around and leaned over the back of the boat. There were four dolphins in all, and they were trailing behind the boat, occasionally leaping up out of the water.

The boat rocked as Ben vibrated with excitement. "Johnny, isn't this cool? Look! They're following us."

Johnny growled and swiped at the air as if he wanted to swat the dolphins away.

"No, no, they're friendly! So friendly, in fact . . . that they've been known to lead adventurers to *treasure*."

Ben eyed Johnny. The zombie boy had been very well behaved on the boat. The pumpkin prevented him from biting anything, and it seemed to weigh him down a little, too. Maybe it would be all right to leave him unattended for a little while.

"You don't mind, do you?" Ben asked, and he pulled a special helmet from his inventory. It was a turtle shell, which he'd made from the scute left behind at Fort Rot. It would allow him to stay underwater longer. He smiled, pleased with his foresight in crafting it at the same time as the boat.

He placed the turtle shell atop his head. "See? Now we both have cool helmets. I'm just going for a little swim. I'll be right back."

Ben hopped out of the boat and into the water. Treading on the surface, he spared a glance back at Johnny. "Stay put!" he said. "Be a good baby, and maybe I'll bring back a treat."

The pumpkin tilted forward, giving Ben the impression that Johnny was nodding. Or maybe the pumpkin was just heavy and had slipped. Either way—he was swimming with dolphins! How great was that?

Ben ducked his head under the water, and it was like a blue curtain lifting to reveal a scene of pure fantasy. Four dolphins swam in playful loops against a backdrop of swaying seaweed and colorful coral. Ben laughed, and bubbles erupted from his open mouth, floating swiftly to the surface.

One dolphin swam up close. Ben reached out to pet it, but the mob ducked away from his hand and swam circles around him. It began to swim off, but stopped and turned to look at him, as if inviting him to follow.

Wait for one second, Ben thought at the dolphin, and he

kicked to the surface to take a breath. Johnny was there, sitting in the boat, just where Ben had left him.

"Good baby," said Ben. "Don't go anywhere!"

And Ben dove once more beneath the waves, determined to follow the dolphin wherever it led him.

CHAPTER 14

Bobbie was staring down the shaft of Flip's crossbow when she realized she would have to do something drastic.

In the past, that had been Ben's job. But Ben wasn't here. And Johnny wouldn't be leaping out to save her this time, either. It was up to Bobbie.

And the truth was, she did have a plan. But it was a terrible, rotten, no-good sort of plan. She needed a better idea.

"So, um, what have you guys been up to?" she said, cleverly stalling for time.

"She's stalling for time," said Hatchet. "Probably thinks she's clever."

"You want me to put some arrows in her?" said Flip. "Make sure she won't be any trouble?"

"I figured we'd take her prisoner." Hatchet smiled. "But there's no reason we couldn't put some holes in her first."

That decided it. Bobbie couldn't afford to stall any longer and hope a better plan occurred to her. It was time to act on the plan she already had.

As Flip chuckled at Hatchet's dark humor, his eyes flicked briefly from Bobbie to Hatchet. That was Bobbie's moment. She darted out of the crossbow's line of fire, pulled the diamond pickaxe from her inventory, and attacked.

She didn't attack Flip or Hatchet, though. She attacked the *fence*. It shattered immediately beneath the force of her blow.

And the zombies surged forward without a moment's hesitation.

This was the part of the plan Bobbie hated the most. She looked back to see how the others would react to the undead breakout. Flip aimed his crossbow at the nearest zombie, and Bobbie gasped.

"Z-zombies!" cried Flip. "They got loose!"

Before Flip could fire an arrow, Hatchet knocked his crossbow aside. "Those are Logan's zombies, idiot! We have to plug the hole and recapture the ones that got loose."

"Right!" said Flip, and he stashed his crossbow so that he could root through his inventory for an appropriate item.

Bobbie didn't wait around to watch the rest. Her distraction had worked perfectly. Hatchet and Flip didn't dare let any harm come to Logan's undead soldiers, and they likewise couldn't allow them to escape. Bobbie had therefore bought herself precious seconds with which to secure her *own* escape, and she didn't intend to waste them.

"I'll be back," she whispered toward the zombies still assembled at the far side of the fence. "I promise." And then she slipped away into the shadows.

As soon as Bobbie was out of sight of Hatchet and Flip, she dug. With her diamond pickaxe, carving a side path off the main tunnel took little effort. She dug forward for a while, then made a hard right turn, and then left, zigging and zagging. It was soon so dark that she couldn't see her hand in front of her face. She went to place a torch . . . and realized her error.

She could dig in random directions all she wanted. But unless she had time to dig false paths and dead ends, then her little escape tunnel would lead her pursuers right to her.

So she dug up.

Gaining the surface, Bobbie ran in a random direction. Without a tunnel to follow, Hatchet and Flip were unlikely to find her again. Even if they split up, the odds were still in Bobbie's favor.

She ran for a long time before she felt safe enough to rest. She leaned against a tree. It was the spruce tree of a taiga biome, not the jungle tree she'd expected. Bobbie scanned the horizon for Logan's outpost tower. The sun was dropping low in the sky, which at least told her which way was west. But did she want to go west or another direction? If she could locate the outpost, she could at least get her bearings, but it was nowhere to be seen.

The sun dipped below the horizon, casting Bobbie's world in deep shadow. And in the dusk, a realization dawned on Bobbie:

She was lost. Entirely, undeniably, *seriously* lost.

In the end, freezing with indecision worked in her favor. As the night's darkness settled over the landscape, an aura of light bloomed on the horizon. At first she thought it was the moon, but when the moon rose and the glow persisted, she realized the light came from an artificial source.

It had to be a village! Bobbie would be safe there, at least for the night. She could rest and resupply and come up with a new plan. She pushed off the tree, running in the direction of that distant glow.

But the night's mobs weren't going to make it that easy for her.

An arrow flew past her, and her first thought was that Flip had found her. But when she turned, she saw something far stranger: a skeletal warrior sitting on top of a spider.

Bobbie quickly hid behind a tree, and the skeleton's next arrow lodged in its trunk. The sight was a reminder to Bobbie: She had a shield in her inventory! She had completely forgotten it when she'd faced the pillager.

As the spider rider scrabbled around for a clear shot, Bobbie quickly searched her inventory. She hoisted the shield up just in time. The skeleton's third arrow found her shield instead of her face.

Despite the fearsomeness of her enemy, she was determined not to panic. The simple act of holding a shield was a comfort, but she knew she couldn't hide behind it forever. Sooner or later, she would have to go on the offensive.

Remembering what Ben had taught her, she decided to move in closer to her enemy. It went against every instinct that she had, but she didn't have enough arrows to fight it at a distance. She counted quietly to herself, and on three, she pushed away from the trunk, rushing toward her foe. She closed the distance quickly, catching the next arrow with her shield as she got into striking range.

The spider would be weaker than the skeleton, she guessed, and it was easier to reach. She attacked it first, unleashing a flurry of hurried slashes, and she laughed in triumph as it burst into dust. The skeleton tumbled to the ground, but it recovered quickly. It fired an arrow at her from point-blank range—there was no way to dodge in time—but her shield held, and she pushed forward with an unrelenting series of blows.

She picked up the bone her fallen adversary left behind. "I'll save this for Johnny," she said, and the allay cooed, reappearing at her side and handing her another apple.

"Uh, thanks," she said. "I guess I could eat."

Layla seemed pleased with that, then darted off—probably to find more apples, Bobbie guessed. It saved her from having to scrounge for food, at least, and allowed her to focus on the task at hand.

A zombie approached her from between the trees, and beyond it, she could hear another spider hissing venomously.

If she wanted to reach that village, she was going to have to fight the whole way.

CHAPTER 15

en had never known he could swim so fast. But as the pod of dolphins darted through the water, he kept up, pausing only to take an occasional breath at the surface.

And then the dolphins dove deep, whistling and chirping as they plunged fearlessly into a vast trench in the seafloor. Ben hesitated briefly, patted his turtle shell for luck, and followed behind.

Ben passed into the trench, deeper than he'd ever gone before. A curtain of seaweed parted, and he saw a sight that threatened to take the last of his breath away.

It was a ship—a vast one, easily ten times the size of the boat he'd crafted. But while Ben's boat floated somewhere above them, this ship would sail no more. Its hull was broken, coral grew in bursts of color up and down its dark wood deck, and though its masts still stood, not even the tattered remnants of sails remained. Ben wondered what great battles this ship might have witnessed.

And he wondered what great riches might have gone down with the ship.

There was a treasure chest on the deck of the ship, visible through the mass of coral. Ben swam forward, alighting on the deck and squeezing through the sharp coral. The light was dim, with sunlight filtering down from high above and tiny, tubelike sea pickles providing low light from the seafloor. Ben decided to grab what he could from the chest and leave immediately.

The chest opened with a creak and an explosion of bubbles. Ben waved the bubbles aside impatiently, eager to see its contents. But the chest held only a few common items: a compass, a clutch of feathers . . . and a map.

Ben grabbed the map for a closer look. The big red X upon it left no doubt—this was a treasure map.

He smiled. It was a real treasure hunt now. And he was up for the challenge.

But as images of emeralds and gold nuggets danced in his mind's eye . . . he very nearly missed the fact that he was not alone. A figure was approaching him through the coral, almost invisible in the dim light.

Ben's first instinct was to greet the figure, but he couldn't speak underwater. He lifted a hand in welcome. Had this treasure map already been claimed . . . ?

But it wasn't another adventurer approaching Ben. It was a monster, with mottled green-gray skin and hair that appeared green with algae. It wore tattered brown clothes and a look of soulless hunger on its face. It was a drowned—an aquatic breed of zombie. It seemed to have been down here in the depths for quite some time.

No wonder it looked hungry.

Ben tried to flee, but there was coral at his back, penning him in. He didn't have time to go around it, so he punched the coral until it broke, clearing a path through which he could retreat.

The drowned wouldn't give him the opportunity. It hefted a trident in its left hand, pulled back its arm, and threw.

The trident sliced into Ben. If not for his armor, he might have been pierced right through his middle. All the same, that had *hurt*. And the drowned wasn't done yet. It was already rearing back for another throw.

Ben prepared to duck, but at this range, he feared it wouldn't do much to protect him. Then he suddenly remembered that he was in water. He could go *up* as well as down!

Ben kicked off the submerged deck, taking to the open water. The second trident missed him, sailing below his feet—but to Ben's dismay, it struck an unsuspecting dolphin.

No! Ben thought, barely remembering to keep his mouth firmly shut.

The dolphins appeared less concerned with staying silent. Every member of the pod chirped with anger as they turned their eyes on the drowned. They darted forward as one, attacking with their pointed snouts as the zombie stabbed back with another trident.

Ben wanted to cheer them on. He wanted to help. But his air was almost up. He needed to head to the surface *now*.

Good luck, fellas, he thought at the pod, then he kicked and stroked, launching himself upward like a firework.

He broke the surface and saw his boat in the middle distance. It was easy to spot on the flat, featureless surface of the water. Swimming over to it, he prepared to hop on board.

But he was greeted with a trident, pointed right at his face.

"Johnny, what's the deal?" he cried, wondering if all zombies suddenly had an endless supply of tridents.

But as he looked up the length of the trident and saw who held it, he realized: "You're not Johnny. What are you doing on my boat?"

"Bad news for ye, lad," said the trident-wielder. Ben saw now that he wore a black hat bearing a white skull—the unmistakable symbol of a pirate. "It's *my* boat now."

CHAPTER 16

obbie had traveled through the night, fighting more than a few mobs along the way. The entire time, she'd been following a light on the horizon, expecting it would lead her to a village.

She was right, mostly. But the village she found was an unusual one. Rather than being wide open and welcoming, this village was shielded against intruders. A great stone wall rose up like the fortification of some storybook castle. Lining the wall was a colorful multitude of banners, each with an unfamiliar sigil, and every three dozen blocks or so, the wall bulged out and up to form a lookout tower made of the same light-gray stone. Just beyond the wall, she could see a multitude of peaked roofs. So people *did* live here, on the other side of the wall. They'd simply taken the defense of their town very seriously.

NICK ELIOPULOS

Bobbie felt her hopes rising with the sun. She'd been alone in the dark for too long. She was ready for some company—and some *help*.

She reached for the gate, but before she could push it open, a voice cried out: "Halt, traveler, and pause! I would know your visit's cause."

"Oh!" said Bobbie, startled. She looked up and saw a figure gazing down on her from the battlements above. "Hi. I'm Bobbie. I'm . . . not from around here. I'm looking for supplies, maybe some directions . . ."

"Ah-ha!" said the figure. "If an adventurer you be, then you may enter—for a fee."

"I'm not an adventurer," said Bobbie. "I'm just a traveler who's . . . who's trying to stop a *bad guy* and overcoming a series of *challenges* along the way . . ." Bobbie heard what she was saying, and she stopped short. "Oh no," she said. "I *am* an adventurer, aren't I?"

Growing up in a village, Bobbie had learned to dislike adventurers. They would breeze through her hometown, take whatever they wanted, and often leave a mess in their wake. Bobbie had never intended to become one herself. But what choice did she have? What was a villager without a village?

"Okay, fine, I'm an adventurer," said Bobbie. "But I'm a *polite* one. I'm just looking for a safe place to rest. There are two other adventurers trying to find me—they're more like mercenaries, really. They and their boss are big trouble."

The figure laughed. "Trouble come is trouble quelled! The Overlords shall ne'er be felled."

"The Overlords?" Bobbie echoed.

"Overworld Overlords is the name of our band. We're the foremost heroes in all the land!"

"Oh, you're rhyming," said Bobbie. "That's nice, but it's not really necessary . . ."

"My name is Kyro, the heroes' bard. I like to rhyme. It isn't hard!"

"Great. Awesome," said Bobbie. She looked over her shoulder, expecting Flip to fire an arrow into her back at any moment. Although . . . this could all have been a tremendous stroke of luck. If these Overlords were as impressive as Kyro said, then even one or two of them might turn the tide in a battle with Logan. Maybe she could hire them? If she'd learned anything from Ben, it was that self-proclaimed heroes loved loot.

Bobbie did a quick mental inventory of her gear. She didn't have much of value. She had a strange totem she'd taken from an evoker that she and Ben had defeated in a woodland mansion, but she doubted that was worth much. Even her precious diamond pickaxe was showing serious signs of wear. Other than that, she had apples. A lot of apples.

Okay, then. She'd have to rely on their sense of honor.

"I have a proposition for the Overlords. Who's in charge around here?" she asked, reaching for the gate.

"Hold!" cried the bard. "Be not so bold!"

Bobbie's skin prickled; she somehow knew what she'd find when she looked up. She lifted her head slowly. The bard was not alone upon the battlements. Several other heroes had appeared, bowstrings drawn and arrows aimed right for Bobbie.

"Okay, okay!" said Bobbie. She raised her hands and took a step backward.

"We have rules. We have tests," said the bard. "If you would enter? Survive a quest."

"What kind of quest?"

"Far below, in the deep dark, a city waits—that is your mark. Within its chests? The echo shard. We'd like a few, if that's not too hard."

Bobbie sighed in frustration. "Okay, so, let me see if I understand this," she said, rubbing her temple. "Before you'll let me come in, I need to dig down into some abandoned city and bring back loot from it. And then you'll let me into your clubhouse, right? And get me an audience with whoever makes the decisions around here?"

"Indeed it's so, and if successful, you will have more than proved your mettle."

Bobbie rolled her eyes. "Fine. Hold that thought. I'll be right back with more echo shards than you'll know what to do with."

The bard cleared his throat. "Yet hark! A warning is only fair. When you go below, of the warden, beware."

Bobbie didn't know what that meant, exactly. But it didn't sound good.

"Thanks for the tip," she said, failing to keep sarcasm out of her voice. "Now off I go. Hurray, pip-pip."

———

"What was that all about?" asked a voice.

Kyro climbed down from the battlements. "An aspiring hero. A would-be friend. You needn't worry about them, Ben."

"I'm glad that you've got such high standards. You can't let just anybody in here with us heroes, right?" Ben grinned with satisfaction. "Now, can I get some more of that cooked chicken? I can't be expected to join the Overlords on an empty stomach!"

CHAPTER 17

Ben had found his way to the Overlords through less conventional means than Bobbie had.

It had all started with an overambitious pirate.

"You can't just steal a person's boat," Ben complained while treading water.

"Of course I can!" said the trident-wielding troublemaker. "I'm Paulie, Prince of Pirates. And stealing boats is what pirates do!"

Paulie certainly looked the part of a pirate, with his black hat and eyepatch, and he wore a tattered fishing net over his clothing, almost like a cape. But this was no grizzled old sea captain. He was a kid, younger than Ben himself, although he was at least a few years older than Johnny.

Wait a minute. Johnny! Where was Johnny?

"What happened to the baby?" Ben demanded.

"What, the little feller with the pumpkin head?" said the pirate. "Booted him overboard, didn't I?"

"You did what?!" Ben cried. "He was just a baby!"

"Ay, well, I be a pirate, and a pirate must be fearsome and— Hey, what are you doing?"

Ben was furious. Batting the trident aside, he pulled himself out of the water and onto the boat. He didn't even bother looking for a weapon. He just clenched his fists and put all his fury into his face.

Paulie flinched. "He's fine! I made sure he was floating before I left him. Honest!" Ben noticed that Paulie had dropped the phony accent.

"You better take me to him," Ben said. "Right now."

"Okay, okay!" said Paulie. He put his trident away and began steering the boat in the right direction. "Gee, you're no fun."

"That baby is my responsibility," said Ben.

"So . . . why'd you leave him alone in a boat in the middle of the ocean?"

Ben didn't have an answer for that. At least not one he cared to share.

They found Johnny within minutes. He was hard to miss, as the oversize pumpkin bobbed atop the water like a big orange signpost.

"Buddy, I am so sorry," Ben said as they approached.

Johnny grumbled.

"I know, I'm terrible," Ben said. "It won't happen again."

NICK ELIOPULOS

"I don't think there's room in this boat for all three of us," said Paulie.

"I'm assuming you can swim," said Ben.

"Come on, this isn't fair!" complained Paulie. He waved his trident around. "I'm a fearsome pirate! You're supposed to give me your stuff!"

"You can have this," said Ben, and he removed the turtle shell from his head. He swiped Paulie's hat and dropped the shell onto the boy's head.

"What's this for?" Paulie asked, tapping the shell.

"It's to make me feel better about doing *this*," Ben answered, and he shoved the boy overboard.

Paulie made a terrific splash, disappearing beneath the water. By the time he'd resurfaced, Ben had already pulled Johnny back on board and steered the ship westward.

"Wait!" said the pirate. "Aren't you forgetting something?" He waved a sheet of tattered paper above the water's surface.

Ben didn't know what it was until he saw the big red X. "You didn't—!" He checked his inventory; the treasure map was gone. "You little sneak!"

"We'll find it together," Paulie promised. "I'm a pirate in need of a crew. You're an adventurer in need of loot!"

"But . . . but this boat isn't big enough for three of us," said Ben. "You said so yourself."

"We can find a nice mooshroom island to stow the baby," Paulie offered.

Johnny mewled, miserable and wet, and Ben looked the baby up and down and sighed. He couldn't really consider leaving Johnny behind. There wasn't a treasure in all the Overworld that would ease his guilt.

"You're wrong about me, Paulie," he said at last. "I'm not just another adventurer. And there are more important things than loot. So you keep that map. I've got everything I need right here in this boat." He patted Johnny's pumpkin affectionately.

The zombie boy growled and swiped at him.

"Come on, Johnny, we're having a moment here," Ben complained.

"Ye'll regret this, landlubber!" cried Paulie, his piratical accent back with a vengeance as he thrashed in the water and stabbed his trident menacingly into the air. "Ye've made a fearsome foe this day. I'll hunt ye to the ends of the Overworld!"

"Yeah, sure," said Ben. "Just be careful where you poke that trident, Paulie. There are some dolphins around here, and they're very quick to anger." He rowed off, calling over his shoulder: "And don't steal any more boats!"

When Ben had taken Paulie's pirate hat, he'd had no idea it would be the key to gaining an audience with the Overworld Overlords.

The coordinates in Logan's journal led to a heavily fortified village, where a strange little fellow dressed somewhat like a jester called down from the battlements: "Look at what the tide's dragged in. I, Kyro, turn thee away, villain."

"Who, me?" said Ben. He wasn't sure at first why he'd been mistaken for a villain, but then he realized that Kyro was eyeing his hat. "Oh, wait, this? No, no. I'm not a pirate." Ben chuckled. "I took this hat off some kid."

Kyro raised an eyebrow. "You stole the vestments of a child? No wonder you're so poorly styled."

"Uh, that's not what I meant," Ben said quickly. He realized he'd better put a more impressive spin on the story. It wasn't a big deal to fib a little bit, right? Every hero did it.

"You didn't let me finish," he said. "I took this hat off some *kidnapper*. That's what I was going to say. A really fearsome pirate with . . . with a crew of skeletons! I beat them all and took their loot."

Kyro's eyes went wide, and for a moment, Ben worried that he'd laid it on too thick. But the bard smiled. "Sounds like you've a tale to tell. I'll let you in, so you need not yell."

Ben turned to Johnny. "Well, that was easy."

"Rawr," said Johnny.

"Back me up in there, all right?" said Ben. "Whatever I say, just go along with it."

"Rawr," Johnny said again.

"Cool cocoa beans," said Ben. "We've got this."

The gate opened, and Kyro was there to greet them, along with two other figures. One was a young woman wearing a set of glittering diamond armor accented with a red cape. The other was a bearded man with no shirt who wielded a glowing pick-axe.

"Kyro tells us you're some sort of pirate slayer," said the woman. "At least, I think that's what he said. The rhyming sometimes makes it hard to follow."

"So she says, but if I could chime in?" said Kyro. "Most folks I meet quite like the rhymin'."

"Keep telling yourself that," said the man. "I'm Major Miner. This is Diamond Jubilee. We're members of—"

"The Overworld Overlords!" Ben finished, awe creeping into his voice. "I know. I've heard about you. I'm Ben. I'm an adventurer like you guys."

"Ha!" said Diamond Jubilee. "We'll be the judge of that, I think."

"And who's the pumpkin-headed fellow? A bit short for an adventurer, isn't he?"

"This is . . . Jack o'Johnny," said Ben. "He's my sidekick." He leaned in closer and whispered: "His true identity is a secret known to only his closest confidants. The pumpkin never comes off in public."

"A man of mystery," said Diamond Jubilee, and her eyes glittered with her armor.

"You certainly have a flair for the dramatic, young fellow," Major Miner said to Johnny. "And a bit of a pungent odor, if you don't mind me saying."

"Oh, right," Ben said quickly. He'd gotten used to Johnny's particular aroma, but these days, the zombie boy certainly smelled more zombie than boy. "He's taken a vow. He refuses to enjoy the comforts of a bath until he enacts vengeance on the villain who . . . um . . . smashed all his pumpkins."

"A vow of grime?" said Diamond Jubilee. "That's a new one."

"Grawr," said Johnny.

"He's . . . also taken a vow of silence?" Ben shrugged.

"Well, Ben, one hero to another?" said Major Miner, and he put an arm around Ben's shoulders. "Don't let your sidekick steal your spotlight. If you want to be in the Overlords someday, you need to show your commitment to a heroic persona. Jack o' has the right idea. Like me—I only do battle with a pickaxe. It *almost* gives the hostile mobs a sporting chance."

He winked, and Ben said, "Wow." Pickaxes weren't well suited to combat, so Major Miner must have tremendous skill.

"Wow is right," said the hero. "You'll find your schtick soon enough, I'm sure. Just don't make the same mistake *she* did." He pointed to Diamond Jubilee. "You should have seen her when they discovered netherite. She wouldn't get out of bed for a week!"

"Diamond used to be the best," she said sadly. "And 'Netherite Jubliee' just doesn't make any sense . . ."

"And then there's this guy." Major Miner pointed to Kyro. "Can you imagine deciding to rhyme nonstop? I'd bet he regrets that he chose that gimmick. I certainly regret it."

Kyro huffed. "Major Miner, I must protest! Many feel rhyming's the best."

"Sure, sure," said the major, and he steered Ben through the gate. "Kyro, why don't you fetch some food for our new friends? Don't bother coming up with a rhyme for 'yes sir,' you can just be on your way. I'll give them the tour."

Kyro stomped off, and Ben, holding firmly to Johnny's lead, allowed himself to be led in turn by Major Miner and Diamond Jubilee.

"We've got quite an operation here, as you can see. Our current roster includes thirteen heroes, who come and go as adventure beckons. We bring back spoils and divide them up. Food, potions, crafting materials . . . everything is communal and shared among us."

Diamond Jubilee sniffed. "Some get a greater share than others, however."

"That's how seniority works, Jubes!" snapped the major. "No more complaining. Now, Ben, that's the cafeteria over there. It doubles as a town hall for important announcements."

Ben recognized the layout of the village. He'd been in a dozen villages just like this one, but the Overlords had clearly made improvements. The stone wall ringing the buildings in an unbroken circle was only the most obvious. As Ben walked the dirt paths, he saw standard wood buildings that had been upgraded with stone expansions and obsidian towers. Covered stone walkways connected several of the buildings, and in the center of town, a squat obsidian structure stood out sharply among the browns and grays of the surrounding buildings.

Ben's overall impression was that the heroes had descended on an average, everyday village, and they had taken enormous liberties to make the village their own personal fortress.

But the villagers were still there. They rushed here and there on their errands, outnumbering the heroes two-to-one.

Major Miner saw him looking. "I know what you're thinking, and no, the villagers aren't members of the order. Think of them as our support staff. They farm and craft, and we take what we need from them. Isn't that right, random villager?" On asking the question, the major reached out to a passing villager, slapping the mob rudely on the side of the head. The villager grumbled in shock and annoyance but kept walking.

"They crack me up," said Major Miner. "Especially when we use them as target practice."

"That's cruel," said Ben, without thinking. As Major Miner and Diamond Jubilee turned to look at him, he felt himself blush.

"They're only villagers," said Diamond Jubilee. "They don't have feelings."

"Are you sure?" said Ben. "I have this friend, Bobbie. She was *raised* by villagers. They took her in when she was just a baby."

"Nonsense," said Major Miner. "People are people, and villagers are just mobs. They're as brainless as chickens or . . . or *zombies*."

Behind them, Johnny growled menacingly.

"Ha!" said Major Miner. "Great zombie impression, kid. That was spot-on."

Zombies, thought Ben. Right. Logan had an army of zombies, and for whatever reason, he was planning to set them loose here. The sun was up now, so they should be safe. But as soon as the sun went down . . .

"Listen," Ben said. "There's a reason I'm here."

"Of course there is!" said the major, putting his arm around Ben once more and pulling him close. Ben sort of wished he'd put on a shirt if he was going to be so touchy. "You're here to join the Overlords!"

"No, I'm— Wait," said Ben, as Major Miner's words sunk in.

"I could—could I really join you all? I mean . . . you'd want me to?"

Ben's heart swelled. He put a lot of stock in being an adventurer. But if he was honest, he hadn't had the best track record lately. And getting dumped by Logan . . . replaced by Other Ben . . . and left behind by Bobbie? It had all left him feeling a little unwanted. The thought of joining the Overlords—and at their invitation? It was almost too good to be true.

"Of course we'd want you to join," said the major. "A triumphant adventurer like yourself? With your very own sidekick? Bane of briny bandits everywhere?" He flicked Ben's pirate hat.

Diamond Jubilee put her fists on her hips. "That's right. You've still got to tell us all about this skeleton pirate crew, you know."

Ben's excitement faded a little. He had, after all, exaggerated his qualifications by a little.

"Oh, leave him alone, Jubes. The details don't matter." Major Miner drew him close. "Now, the initiation fee is really quite reasonable. How many emeralds do you have on you now?"

Ben's heart, already deflating, fell into his stomach. "There's a *fee* to join?"

"A nominal fee," said the major. "Just enough to know you're legit. And the monthly dues are much cheaper if you pay up front."

"But when you bring in new recruits, you get to keep a portion of their fee." Diamond Jubilee shrugged. "It ends up paying for itself, if you can find the right recruits."

"Tell you what, Bandit Ben." Major Miner smiled. "Yeah, you like the sound of that name, don't you? How about you stick around for a bit. Eat of our food, sleep in whatever bed's free, and give us your answer in the morning. How does that sound?"

"Hello and hi, did someone say food?" said Kyro as he stepped out of the building that Major Miner had identified as the cafeteria. "I've some cooked chicken, if you're in the mood."

Ben's mouth watered. He couldn't remember the last time he'd had a hot meal that he hadn't prepared himself. He could get used to this.

"Thanks, Kyro," he said around a mouthful of tender chicken. "This is awesome—all of this. The Overlords are everything I dreamed they'd be." Ben shook his head. "But that only makes my business here more urgent. The real reason I'm here is to warn you: You're all in terrible danger."

Kyro laughed. "Danger is our middle name. We fear no evil. We fear no pain."

"Did that rhyme?" asked Major Miner.

"Slant rhyme," answered Diamond Jubilee. She shrugged. "It counts."

"Please, listen," said Ben. "There's this guy, this . . . this *villain*, I guess. His name's Logan, and he's coming here to attack this place."

"Ah!" Kyro nodded. "Logan, he is known to us. He wished to join; we said, get lost."

"That explains it," said Ben. "Logan isn't the kind of guy to forgive and forget. He must be out for revenge."

"Then he should have paid the fee," said Diamond Jubilee.

"We do have standards, you know," said Major Miner. "But I don't think we have anything to fear from Logan. If nothing else, we have him handily outnumbered."

They were wrong there. Of course, they didn't know about the army of zombies. Warning them now would give them a chance to prepare.

Only . . . even if they believed him . . . wouldn't that just mean that the heroes would destroy the zombies? That was the opposite of what Bobbie wanted to happen. She had friends and family members in that zombie horde.

"You need to evacuate," he said. "Fighting this threat would be . . . impossible. The things Logan has planned? Really super scary! You've got to get out of here. Maybe relocate to a tropical biome? I bet the jungle is lovely this time of year."

"Ha!" said Kyro. "To think that we would turn and flee? What sort of heroes would we then be?"

"You have to admit, we've got a pretty sweet setup here," said Major Miner. "If somebody comes for us, we'll defend this place like our lives depend on it."

"I feel sorry for anyone who'd try to take what's ours," said Diamond Jubilee.

"Yeah. Yeah, me too," said Ben, and his heart sank. If he couldn't convince the Overlords to avoid Logan's attack, then they were in for the fight of their lives. And whichever side won, the casualties were going to be tragic. Ben was just glad Bobbie wouldn't be here to witness it.

Although Bobbie wouldn't give up so quickly, would she? She'd find some way to convince the Overlords to hear her out. She wouldn't take no for an answer!

And maybe she'd eat a lot of free food while she worked on a solution? Hard to say, but Ben certainly wasn't going to be shy. "Is there any more of that chicken, Kyro? I do my best thinking on a full stomach."

"In a moment, I will fetch some more," said Kyro, and at a signal from a fellow Overlord stationed atop the battlements, he hurried back toward the gate. "Right now, I must see who's at the door!"

CHAPTER 18

Bobbie couldn't believe it when Kyro sent her away. What sort of village made a traveler prove herself worthy before they'd let her inside?

Although, come to think of it, her village might have fared better with a similar policy. She was the one who'd welcomed Logan in with open arms, after all. And that had gone exceedingly poorly.

Whatever. If Bobbie had to run some random errand in order to earn her way inside, she would do it. She had a very strong suspicion that Hatchet and Flip were just a few steps behind her. And she was beginning to think she would need all the help she could get against Logan. Leaving Ben behind had not been her all-time best idea.

Bobbie allowed her frustration—at Kyro, at Logan, at herself—to fuel every swing of her pickaxe. She carved an irregular staircase into the ground, cutting through grass, then dirt, then seemingly endless layers of stone. Eventually her tunnel connected with an open pocket of subterranean space. It was a cavern, and, judging by the warm orange light that illuminated its craggy corners, she knew what she'd find there: lava.

She proceeded carefully. She hadn't seen much lava in her lifetime, and while she found it fascinating, she was also a little scared of it. The idea that she could take one false step and literally burst into flames was not a comforting thought.

But the light would keep monsters from spawning in the cavern, and the bright swirling colors of the lava were almost hypnotically beautiful, particularly where the lava was pouring into the chamber, like a miniature lavafall. She allowed herself a moment of rest, searching the lava's shapes for patterns—maybe even a sign of some sort—but all she saw was chaos.

She sighed. To find the loot she was looking for, she'd have to dig deeper still. But the last thing she wanted was to dig a hole in the wrong place and have a torrent of lava follow her down. A lavafall was pretty . . . until it was coming down on your head. She would have to be careful about where she cut her next hole. And she'd have to provide her own light from here.

She dug through her inventory and found she had only a handful of torches left. And though she had picked up plenty of coal while digging, she'd used up nearly every scrap of wood she'd been carrying around.

She didn't like her chances of finding wood underground. So as much as it bothered her to lose the time, she decided to retrace her steps back to the surface. Since the path was already cut, it would be faster going up than it had been coming down.

A few moments later, she was on the surface, cutting into trees for all the wood she'd need. The forest trees were abundant, and rabbits and chickens went about their business. Her surroundings were peaceful, and the action of chopping trees was relaxing, and soon Bobbie had let her guard down entirely.

It was then that she heard the voices she'd dreaded hearing.

"I'm sure she went this way," said Flip.

"That's what you said last time," Hatchet complained.

"Well, by process of elimination . . ."

Hatchet growled. "Just keep an eye out for any sign that someone's been this way."

Bobbie froze. She looked around her, at the little grove where she'd been gathering wood. A dozen trees were partially hacked away, their stumps an unmistakable sign of human activity.

Hatchet and Flip would see this grove, and they would know that Bobbie had been here.

She hurried back to her hole, which she'd dug next to a river. Once underground, she used dirt to plug the entrance, so that Hatchet and Flip wouldn't see it—the lava light glowing from below would be especially obvious as the sun went down. But would they notice the naked patch of dirt in a field of grass and flowers?

Bobbie worried she'd left behind too obvious a trail. Should she close off the tunnel behind her? Did she have *time* for that?

Maybe she could flood it instead.

Acting almost on impulse, Bobbie used her diamond pickaxe to dig sideways, toward the nearby river. She soon struck water. It rushed forward to fill the hole, surging into her little tunnel and knocking her back. The torrent of water followed the path she'd cut in the earth, rushing down and taking her with it.

Bobbie laughed. She'd created a waterslide! If not for the enemies above her and the lava below, she would have been content to lie back and enjoy the ride.

But she fought the current, careful not to let it sweep her into the lava pool below. Once in the cavern, she quickly found her footing, hopping onto a dry patch of stone in a corner.

Where water met lava, shiny new blocks of obsidian had formed.

Bobbie looked at her diamond pickaxe. It was strong enough to allow her to harvest the obsidian blocks. It would be a little risky, cutting that close to flowing lava, while fighting the current of the water. But if she was careful, she could gather quite a fair bit of obsidian.

And obsidian would be useful . . . for setting a trap.

Once Bobbie had what she needed from the flooded cavern, she walled off the water, prepared her torches, and dug. She didn't stop digging until she hit bedrock. It was as deep as she'd ever been.

She dug to the side, and up a bit, because her intended trap

would require some room to maneuver. Sooner than she'd expected, she cut through a final wall of stone, and her fresh-
carved staircase opened on a vast, cavernous hollow. Emerging
from her narrow tunnel of stone, she found it hard to wrap her
mind around the scale of the place. She could scarcely see the
ceiling of stone that she knew was high above, and the stony
shapes in the distance had a distinctly crafted quality. There was
even a wooden tower, not unlike the one the pillagers had used
as an outpost.

So this wasn't a natural cavern, then. Not entirely. Someone
had *made* this.

"Ancient city," said Bobbie. "Found it!"

A plantlike growth nearby seemed to react to her voice, emit-
ting eerie blue circles in the air. Almost at the same time, a
shrieking sound rang out. At first, she thought Flip and Hatchet
had found her. But this sound—it was *inhuman*. And was she
imagining it, or was her vision darkening, too? Bobbie flinched
and crouched low, certain that some unknown mob was ready-
ing an attack. The bard had mentioned something called a warden . . .

But as Bobbie looked all around, she saw the source of the
sound wasn't a mob at all, but another one of the strange, glowing plantlike blocks that appeared irregularly throughout the
area. Bobbie whacked it with her pickaxe until it broke, and the
noise immediately fell silent.

Bobbie sighed in relief. That had been annoying, but it
hadn't seemed to have caused any harm. Nothing was around to

hear the noise, and she'd silenced it quickly. She got to work digging. She needed to set her trap before Hatchet and Flip—or something even worse—found her alone down here.

Despite the darkness, no zombies or skeletons or creepers appeared to challenge her. That, at least, was a relief. The darkness itself was heavy but not absolute. There were strange blue lanterns set about, and toward the center of the cavern, a stronger blue light seemed to beckon her. She suspected that any loot worth looting would be found in that direction.

As she walked, the area seemed more and more fortresslike, with the blue lanterns highlighting castlelike battlements and more of the outpostlike wooden towers. All empty, to her relief. There was faded carpeting along some of the otherwise stony ground. When she came to a stretch of wool blocks, walking upon it made her feel like a ghost, utterly silent and detached from her surroundings. She stepped to the side, preferring the natural stonework to the eerily soft and silent wool.

A second shrieking block activated. Bobbie thought the cavern grew even darker at the same time. She struggled to find the source of the noise, nearly tripping over the shrieker. She silenced it with a few deft swings.

She thought she heard the faintest sound of a heartbeat, and a trilling noise in the distance. But then all was silent. Clearly, her imagination was getting the better of her.

But she stayed on the wool floor after that. Maybe being silent down here wasn't the worst idea.

In the silence, however . . . the hairs on the back of her neck stood up as she got the unnerving sense that someone was watching her.

She turned to look back the way she'd come. She'd left some torches along the path, so that it would be easier to retrace her steps when she was finished exploring—Ben had taught her that. Of course, it would also make it easier to be followed . . .

In the middle distance, Bobbie saw a dark figure step in front of a torch.

She wasn't alone down here. The question was, had Flip and Hatchet caught up to her? Or was it a hostile mob, shuffling aimlessly in the dark, blocking her path back to the surface by sheer luck?

Bobbie wasn't taking any chances. She pulled out her crossbow and pointed it in the direction of the figure. It was a little too far away, and much too dim, to see with any detail. But if it passed in front of another torch, giving away its position . . .

There! Bobbie let the arrow fly, just as the figure became outlined in hazy torchlight. She held her breath, waiting to discover if her aim had been true.

The sound of her crossbow set off another shrieking plant, back behind her somewhere. She ignored it, keeping her focus on the battle ahead of her.

A shouted "Ow!" told her two things. One, her aim was true as could be.

And two . . . this was not some mindless mob. It was a *person* who had made that sound.

Hatchet and Flip had found her at last.

Bobbie knew there was no way she could win a battle against the two of them. Especially not down here in the dark. But she had a plan, and for the plan to work, she needed them to follow her.

"There's more where that came from!" Bobbie cried. "Better catch me."

"Wait!" whispered the figure in the dark. "Shush!"

"I said come and get me!" Bobbie cried, and she fired another arrow in the figure's direction.

That did the trick. Bobbie saw the shadowy figure whip by another torch, coming her way in a hurry. She turned and ran, looping through tall columns of stonework so that she could get to the far side of the figure. She needed to follow the torchlit path—and she needed her pursuer to follow her.

Within moments, Bobbie saw the hole she had left in the ground, but only because she knew to look for it. She leaped over it handily.

Her pursuer was not so lucky. She heard the figure tumble into the hole and land on the bedrock below with a painful thud. "Ow!" they cried again.

She'd caught only one of them, though. Was it Hatchet or Flip? It hardly mattered. The pit she'd dug was lined with obsidian. They'd be hard pressed to cut their way out, and *climbing* out would take no small amount of time. Especially once Bobbie plugged the hole, plunging her captive into utter darkness.

She doubled back to the pit. "Enjoy your stay," said Bobbie. "It's better than you deserve."

"Harsh," said her captive. "I thought we were friends!"

Bobbie couldn't believe her ears. She dropped the block she was holding and fumbled around for a torch. By the light it cast, she could finally see the figure she'd caught in her trap.

It wasn't Hatchet. It wasn't Flip.

"Ben?!" she cried. "What are *you* doing here?"

CHAPTER 19

Although their reunion wasn't going quite as he'd pictured it, Ben was genuinely happy to see Bobbie—even if he was looking up at her from the bottom of a dark, creepy pit.

"Believe it or not, I'm here to save you," Ben told her, rubbing his aching head, which he'd hit against a block of obsidian when he'd fallen. "Despite what it may look like. You know me, I can't resist a daring rescue."

"As rescues go, I've seen better," said Bobbie. "But it's really good to see you, Ben. Only—where's Johnny?" She looked over her shoulder. "You didn't bring him down here, did you?"

"Relax," Ben answered. "Johnny's safe. I left him with the Overlords."

Bobbie slapped her forehead. "You left my brother the zombie in the care of professional monster hunters?"

"Well, it sounds bad when you put it that way," Ben said. "But he barely even looks like a zombie when he's wearing the pumpkin. I promise, he's completely safe. I learned my lesson when the pirate threw him— Actually, never mind. Are you going to help me up?"

Bobbie tossed a stack of dirt blocks into the hole. Ben saw what she had in mind. He was able to build a simple dirt column right beneath his feet. He was back on her level in no time.

"It *is* good to see you," said Bobbie, and she leaned in for a hug. "And it's *great* to know my trap worked."

"Happy to help," he said, leaning into her hug. Then he pulled away and looked into her eyes. "Listen, Bobbie, you're in danger down here. And a hole in the ground isn't going to be much help against a warden."

"What is a warden, exactly?" asked Bobbie. "I thought I'd seen every hostile mob in the Overworld by this point."

"Not even close. Remind me to tell you about the zombie pig monster."

Bobbie crossed her arms. "Now you're just making up stories."

"Shh!" said Ben. "Let's try to keep quiet, all right? You haven't set off any of the shriekers, have you?"

Bobbie shrugged. "Yeah. A few of them."

Ben's blood went cold. "A few?" he said. "How many is a 'few'?"

"Two or three? I don't know." Bobbie threw her hands up. "Anyway, whatever a warden is, I'm more worried about Logan's cronies. Hatchet and Flip are looking for me as we speak."

"Looking," said a voice.

"And finding," said another.

Ben knew what he'd see as he whirled around. Hatchet stepped from the shadows, her axe glinting in the low torchlight, and Flip was right behind her, aiming his crossbow in their direction.

"We'd just about given up on finding you," said Hatchet.

"You're good at covering your tracks," added Flip.

"Flip!" said Hatchet. "Don't compliment the enemy."

"Wasn't a compliment," said Flip. "I was complaining! Don't like being led on a wild squid chase."

"Fortunately we saw your little friend running around." Hatchet pointed her hatchet at Ben. "He led us right to you."

"Oops," said Ben.

"Wait," said Bobbie, turning to Ben. "How did *you* find me?"

"Kyro told me he'd sent some snarky adventurer-who-says-she's-not-an-adventurer down here on a quest that was almost certain to kill her." Ben shrugged. "I figured he was talking about you."

"Kyro!" said Bobbie. "I knew he was bad news."

"Excuse me," said Flip. "I'd like to think the guy with the crossbow aimed at your head is all the bad news you need."

"You two caused us a lot of trouble," said Hatchet. "You know Logan blamed *us* for all that chaos back at Fort Rot? But when we bring him your heads, he'll take us back with open arms."

"Good plan," said Bobbie. "One problem, though. It wasn't just the two of us who caused that trouble. Right, Ben?"

Bobbie elbowed Ben in the side. He wasn't sure what she was

up to, but he recognized that she needed him to play along. "Right," he said. "You forgot about the third member of our team. Her brother, the zombie."

"You remember him, don't you? Get 'em, Johnny!"

Hatchet and Flip whirled around, expecting a pint-sized zombie to come lunging out of the shadows.

Ben wanted to applaud Bobbie's cleverness, but there was no time. She grabbed his hand and pulled him after her. He hoped she could see better than he could. Even with the torches, it was unnaturally dark down here. For all he knew, he might be about to put his foot into another hole.

"Hey!" Hatchet called after them. "Flip, shoot them!"

"I can't even see 'em!" complained Flip. "Come on, after them!"

Ben heard their footsteps giving chase.

"I assume you have a plan?" Ben asked.

"I had a great plan!" she said. "Lure them into a pit. It was going to be glorious!"

"I'm not going to apologize for falling into your trap!" said Ben. "In fact, any time *you'd* like to apologize to *me*, I'm ready and—"

Ben didn't finish the sentence. It was impossibly dark, and he tripped over some object on the ground. It was a sculk shrieker—the *last* thing he wanted it to be.

The shrieker let off a horrible, earsplitting noise, giving away their location.

"Over there!" yelled Hatchet.

Suddenly, the sound of shifting earth and breaking rocks

filled the cavern. The ground at Bobbie's feet churned, as if something were burrowing its way up from below. She took a few faltering steps back, pulling Ben to his feet, and together they watched as a figure broke through the surface and pulled itself up to its full, terrifying height. It was massive, but indistinct—a deeper darkness amid the shadow. Ben thought he could just make out the gaping black hollow of a mouth in an otherwise featureless face.

The warden was here. And Ben knew they didn't stand a chance.

CHAPTER 20

The creature that loomed before them was easily the most frightening thing Bobbie had ever laid eyes on. It didn't help that darkness seemed to have settled upon them as the creature had raised itself from the ground. It was well and truly dark now, despite the torches and lanterns. She wanted nothing more than to run, but her feet felt like blocks of iron.

"Is that a *warden*?" whispered Bobbie.

Ben gestured furiously for her to be quiet, but he also sort of nodded wildly.

I'll take that as a yes, thought Bobbie. It was obvious that Ben found the warden every bit as horrifying as she did.

Hatchet and Flip evidently agreed.

"Wh-wh-what is that?" cried Flip.

The creature was so close Bobbie could have reached out and touched it if she wanted to. (She didn't want to.) But it spun around at the sound of Flip's voice. It seemed to sniff the air, as if it could smell them but not see them. Was it blind? Did it even know she was here?

Bobbie sighed loudly in relief, then quickly covered her mouth. Too late—the warden whirled back in her direction, sniffing furiously.

Flip's crossbow went off, although Bobbie couldn't say whether he'd fired it on purpose. It was too dark to see the arrow, but the sound of the crossbow was enough to once more attract the warden's attention.

The creature roared, stalking toward the others. Bobbie fumbled for Ben's hand and, when she found it, she gripped it tightly. She knew this was their opportunity to flee. But it was so dark! Where was the exit? She floundered, tripping over a block.

But Ben caught her as she fell.

"Don't panic," he whispered as quietly as possible. "We can survive this, if we stick together."

"Maybe," said Bobbie. "Can they?"

As if on cue, Hatchet and Flip screamed.

"Get it! Shoot it!" cried Hatchet.

"I did!" said Flip. "It didn't even—"

The warden roared, and Flip went careening back into the wall. Bobbie hadn't seen the creature strike him. She had no idea the full extent of its abilities, and she didn't care to find out.

She allowed Ben to pull her in the opposite direction, deeper into the ancient city. Dark columns loomed above them, and Bobbie ducked behind one for cover.

"We can't just leave them," Bobbie whispered.

"Uh, yes, we can," Ben whispered back.

"Ben! That thing will destroy them."

"What if I promise to host a very tasteful memorial service?" At Bobbie's withering look, Ben sighed. "*Fine*. You know, I forgot how bossy you are."

"You say bossy," said Bobbie. "I say natural leader." She pulled her crossbow from her inventory. She had only a couple of arrows left.

"I don't think that's going to do much damage," Ben warned.

"I agree," said Bobbie. "But I'm hoping it'll make some noise."

Bobbie set the arrow loose, aiming in the direction of a sculk sensor block. Her plan was a simple one: activate the sensor with an arrow, setting off a shrieker that would draw the creature's attention and allow Hatchet and Flip to sneak away.

But she was too close, and her crossbow was too loud. The warden whirled away from Hatchet and Flip, as she'd hoped. But it seemed to draw a bead on her instead.

"Run!" Ben hissed. "Come on!"

This time, Bobbie didn't resist. She let him pull her toward the heart of the city. The empty battlements looked down on them, making Bobbie feel strangely exposed. Anything could be up there, watching, lying in wait.

But at the sound of sniffing, she knew the true threat was behind her. Closer than she'd like.

Ben chose an open doorway at random. Bobbie heard the click of a pressure plate, and a hidden compartment slid open.

They both dove through the opening, which slid shut behind them.

The room was pitch-dark. They huddled together, trying not to make a sound. Bobbie counted to thirty. She began to think they might be safe.

There was sniffing at the door.

Bobbie gasped, and the warden roared. Ben cut through the far wall, and eerie blue light flooded into the room, just as the warden burrowed up once more from the ground.

They emerged in what felt like a central area, almost like a courtyard, but with an imposing ring structure looming above them like a monument. It looked to Bobbie almost like a gaping maw—or a dead portal, lit from below by a bed of blue flame.

Ben dove for a treasure chest.

"Really?" she said. "Now?"

"There might be something—!" he said, and then, raising a stack of snowballs into the air, he cried, "Aha!"

The warden rounded a corner, roaring.

"Up!" said Ben. "Build!"

But Bobbie was busy staring inside the open chest.

"An echo shard!" she cried, grabbing the item.

"I thought now wasn't the time for looting?" Ben asked.

"I'll explain later." Bobbie began laying blocks in a staircase pattern as quickly as she could. The warden approached steadily, but within moments, they were high enough to be out of its immediate reach. Ben broke the blocks behind them, leaving them on a floating platform. But were they safe?

Ben handed her a few snowballs, and she saw what he had in

mind: a variation on her idea from before. But snowballs would be much quieter than a crossbow.

She threw one as far as she could manage. It hit a far wall with a splat, and the warden turned in that direction.

Ben threw another snowball in the same direction. The warden roared, then stalked toward the sound it had heard, sniffing the air.

They squeezed close together on their little platform, straining their eyes to track the creature's movements. When it failed to find anyone where the sound of snowballs had led it, it paced the area, sniffing furiously.

But they must have been beyond the range of its senses. Eventually, the warden seemed to give up its pursuit, burrowing back into the ground beneath its feet. Even then, Bobbie and Ben waited long minutes in silence, neither wanting to be the first to make a sound.

In the end, they exchanged a nod, and Bobbie led the way, placing blocks to bring them back to ground level. They stuck to the wool floor whenever possible and ignored the chests they passed along the way.

When they'd reached Bobbie's tunnel, lined with torches that would lead all the way to the surface, they thought they were safe. To Bobbie's immense disappointment, two familiar faces were waiting to greet them midway between bedrock and daylight.

"There they are," said Hatchet. "Now we can get back to business." Bobbie saw that Flip was already pointing his crossbow at her.

"Are you serious?" said Bobbie. "We just saved your lives!"

Flip grinned. "And when Logan hears that we got rid of you, you'll have saved our reputations, too."

"I've had about enough of this," said Ben. "Bobbie— maneuver nineteen!"

Bobbie had no idea what "maneuver nineteen" was, but as Ben lunged forward to knock Flip's crossbow aside, she swung her diamond pickaxe down, right onto Hatchet's foot.

Hatchet screamed in shock and pain, and Flip dropped his crossbow to put his hands over her mouth. "Hey, quiet down!" he said. "That thing's still down there somewhere!"

Ben grabbed Flip's crossbow, grinning at Bobbie. "That wasn't maneuver nineteen, but it worked!"

Hatchet pushed Flip away and gripped her axe. "If you think you've got us beat—"

"Oh, stop it," said Bobbie. "You two are injured, and you have no room to maneuver. And Ben and I make a great team— it's not two against one anymore."

"And!" added Ben. "You're fighting for all the wrong reasons. Logan doesn't want you two around. Beating up Bobbie and me won't change that." He extended a book in their direction. "Go on. See for yourself."

Hesitantly, as if she expected it was some kind of trap, Hatchet took the book from Ben. "What is this?" she asked, flipping through the pages.

"It's Logan's journal," answered Ben. "And it isn't pretty. But I needed to see the truth, and so do you." Ben shrugged. "Logan's not a nice person."

Flip scoffed. "You're just saying that cause he dumped you."

"I'll admit it: It hurt my feelings when Logan left me behind." Ben's shoulders slumped. "I thought we were friends. *Partners.* I thought he saw past my shortcomings and wanted to spend time with me anyway." He shook his head. "But he was keeping a list of my shortcomings. Judging me the whole time. Using me until I was no longer useful to him. And he was doing the same to you two."

Flip looked over Hatchet's shoulder.

"Is that supposed to be a drawing of *me?*" said Flip. "I never wore a dunce cap in my life!"

"He kept a tally of every time you missed a target," Hatchet said. "And look: He has a whole page where he lists foolish stuff I said!"

"Two pages," Ben said, and when Hatchet floundered, Ben said, "No, no, you're supposed to read books left to right . . ."

"That . . . that total slime!" she cried, and she threw the book to the ground. "After all we did for him. He'd be nothing without us!"

"We gathered most of his army for him," said Flip. "We fought whoever he said to fight, and we gave him all the cool loot we found. We even guarded his fort while he went off on his great adventure!"

"Well," Ben said, "you didn't do a *great* job of that last thing."

"Logan was right about one thing," said Hatchet. She turned to Flip. "We haven't been very smart, have we? Why'd we let him boss us around, anyway? We've got everything we need, between the two of us."

Flip sighed in relief. "If I'm perfectly honest with you, Hatchet, I was not looking forward to fighting the Overworld Overlords."

"Right?" Hatchet said. "He thinks he's so smart? He can handle the Overlords by himself."

"Yeah." Flip nodded. "If they don't stop him, Pigstep Peggy will."

"Logan is going after the Overworld Overlords? That's news to me," said Bobbie. "And who is Pigstep Peggy?"

Hatchet scoffed. "She's the one who taught the Overlords everything they know. If Logan thinks he's going to take her down without a fight, he's in for a surprise."

"You could join us, you know," said Ben. "Together, we could stop him before he hurts anyone else."

"Nah," Hatchet said. "We've wasted enough time on this nonsense. We've got life goals of our own, you know."

"Like getting rich," said Flip. "Fighting zombies never got anybody rich."

"Yeah," Ben said wistfully. "Tell me about it."

Bobbie smacked his shoulder. "Priorities, Ben!"

"But we won't stand in your way no more," said Flip. "And if you want to know the truth . . . I'm rooting for you."

"Hey, thanks, Flip," Bobbie said, smiling.

"Me, I kind of hope you all kill each other," said Hatchet. "Who knows? Wishes can come true."

On that cheery note, Hatchet and Flip began cutting an upward-sloping path through the stone. Bobbie hoped they'd seen the last of them, but she doubted it.

"Should we let them go?" she asked Ben. "They're bound to cause someone trouble."

"I'm not sure we could stop them if we wanted to," said Ben. "Besides, we have enough problems." He smiled. "Now come on. I know a certain zombie who's un-dying to see you."

CHAPTER 21

The sun was close to the horizon when they reached the surface. After so long in the deep dark, Ben thought even the dim light of dusk felt almost overpowering. He blinked against the brightness.

"I'm all turned around," said Bobbie.

"There," said Ben, pointing. "I left a trail of torches. If we follow them, we'll reach the Overlords' headquarters before dark."

"And then what?" Bobbie said, trailing just behind him. "We can't let Logan demolish them, but . . ."

"But we also can't let the Overlords decimate the zombies," Ben finished. "I know. That's what I was trying to figure out before I rushed off to find you." He shook his head. "The heroes I talked to were not very worried about Logan. But they did kind of . . . sort of . . ." He stopped walking and turned to face her.

"They offered to let me join them. They said I could be an Over-world Overlord!"

"Oh!" said Bobbie. She was obviously surprised by the news. "Is that . . . something you'd want?"

Ben couldn't suppress a grin. "I mean, it would be kind of amazing, wouldn't it?"

Ben started walking again, and Bobbie fell into step beside him. "You know me. I'm suspicious of people who go around calling themselves *heroes*." She shrugged. "And Kyro the Bard apparently doesn't care if I live or die, sending me into warden territory like he did. But if being in a guild would be good for your career . . ."

"Yeah. I mean, not now, obviously," Ben said quickly. "First I'm going to help you get the zombies cured. And that would give me some time to get the initiation fee together."

"There's a fee?"

"Yeah, and dues . . . but I can actually *make* money if I bring in new recruits. Maybe you'd want to join?"

"For . . . a fee," said Bobbie.

Ben nodded, smiling happily.

"It . . . sounds a little suspicious," said Bobbie. "Don't you think?"

Ben felt his smile falter. "What do you mean?"

Bobbie shrugged. "Nothing. Maybe it's nothing." She scratched her head. "But, you know, be careful. The heroes who used to come through my village . . . sometimes they cared more about loot than people."

Ben sighed theatrically. "I know, I know. You don't trust heroes. But these ones are different. They're literally the best."

"Right." Bobbie nodded. "Although Kyro sort of sent me off to certain death."

"Not so certain!" Ben argued. "You survived."

Bobbie shrugged again.

"You think they're con artists," Ben said hotly. "You think they're trying to trick me out of my hard-earned emeralds."

"Your words," said Bobbie. "I only said to be careful."

"Unbelievable," said Ben. He gave her a long look. "And you're sure you're not just jealous?"

Bobbie gave him a look of pure pity. "You're a brilliant adventurer, Ben. They should be paying *you*. Not the other way around."

"But they're famous," argued Ben. "You know who I saw in the cafeteria? Iron Aaron! He's been to the End and back without ever upgrading his armor!"

"That sounds needlessly reckless," said Bobbie.

"It sounds awesome!" countered Ben. "Trust me. Kyro's a little sketchy, but the rest of them? Once you meet them, you'll get it. We'll help them stop Logan. They'll help us cure the zombies. And then we'll bask in triumph and glory as the most famous heroes of the Overworld sing songs about our valor and carry us around on their shoulders!"

Bobbie gave him a look. This time it was *not* a look of pity but of judgment.

"The first two things being the more important part, naturally," Ben said quickly.

Kyro the Bard greeted them at the gates of the walled village. "Hail and welcome! But I must ask." He leaned over the ramparts. "Was the girl successful in her task?"

"*The girl's* name is Bobbie, as I'm sure you'll remember." She held up a shard. "And I'd call this successful. Wouldn't you?"

In response, Kyro gave a signal, and the gate swung open. Major Miner was there to greet them. "Bandit Ben!" he cried in greeting. "Have you found another sidekick already?"

"Is he talking about me?" asked Bobbie. She leaned close to Major Miner. "I'm nobody's sidekick, buddy. Now, who's in charge around here?"

Major Miner turned to Ben. "No vow of silence for this one, eh?"

Bobbie obviously didn't like the sound of that. She opened her mouth, preparing to deliver some sort of retort.

But a great horn sounded, interrupting Bobbie and drawing the attention of everyone around them.

"What is that?" she said.

"A raid horn has sounded!" Kyro shouted down from the ramparts. "We're about to get pounded!"

"Get that gate shut!" Major Miner yelled up at the bard. Then he turned back to Ben. "You must have the mark of bad omen. Did you recently strike down a pillager captain?"

"Me? No!" said Ben. "Believe me, if I had, I'd be bragging about it."

"Uh," said Bobbie, raising her hand meekly. "I defeated a

couple of pillagers recently. It was at a wooden tower thing, like an outpost? I don't know if any of them was a captain . . ."

Ben's eyes went wide. "You fought against pillagers? And won?!"

"To arms!" cried Kyro. "We're about to be invaded!"

"That didn't even rhyme," Bobbie complained.

"Come on!" Ben said, and he climbed the ladder to the ramparts. Bobbie followed close behind.

From Kyro's perch atop the wall, by the fading light of the sun, Ben and Bobbie had a view of the invasion's opening moments. "There!" shouted one of the heroes atop the wall, and Ben saw a pillager appear from behind a tree and fire an arrow in their direction.

"And over there!" said Bobbie, as she pointed out a second approaching pillager.

"Watch it," warned Ben, and he ducked a third pillager's arrow.

"Return fire!" cried a hero, and all those assembled atop the wall launched arrows at the invaders. Ben and Bobbie joined in, using their crossbows. The trio of pillagers fell to the onslaught of arrows before they'd even reached the gate.

"That wasn't so bad," said Bobbie.

Suddenly, a tremendous crash sounded from nearby, and vibrations shook the wall. Ben and Bobbie turned to see that the wall had been breached on the far side of the village. Pillagers came streaming in through the gap.

Bobbie aimed her crossbow, but Ben put his hand on her

elbow. "Wait," he said. "It's too far. And you might hit one of *them*."

As they watched, heroes leaped into action. Major Miner led the charge, with his softly glowing pickaxe. Diamond Jubilee fought by his side.

"See?" said Ben. "They're the real deal—adventurers, not con artists."

"They can be both," Bobbie insisted. "But Ben, where's Johnny? If he's caught in the middle of this . . ."

"I'll take you to him," said Ben, and he hopped back onto the ladder. "Follow me!"

Ben led Bobbie through the village. For now, the fighting was contained to the perimeter. Heroes ran toward the chaos, and villagers fled from it, returning to their dwellings.

And then the sun set, and Bobbie abruptly stopped running.

"Do you hear that?" she asked.

"Hear what?" Ben replied, and he strained to listen.

Bobbie was right. There was a strange and urgent sound, just barely audible beneath the noise of battle.

Literally beneath it.

"Digging," he said, and his mouth dropped open. "Someone is digging up from underground! If the warden followed us . . ."

"Not the warden," Bobbie said, and she grimaced. "Curse it. He was waiting for the sun to go down. Logan is here!"

The ground near their feet crumbled. A gaping hole spread halfway across the village. And from that great crack in the earth arose an endless stream of zombies. Logan's assault had begun — at the worst possible moment.

In the distance, Diamond Jubilee was leading a group of heroes in combat against the pillagers and vindicators who had breached the wall. She never heard the zombies approaching from behind. When one of them swiped at her, she turned, and her eyes went wide with realization: The heroes were trapped between two invading armies.

Ben saw Major Miner surreptitiously swap his pickaxe for a sword. So much for his commitment to his brand.

Nearby, Kyro yelped in shock. Ben turned in time to watch the bard lash out at an undead attacker who had struck him in the back.

"Don't hurt them!" cried Bobbie. "They don't know what they're doing!"

"I don't think they're going to listen," Ben said.

"Then we've got to end this battle right now," Bobbie said. "But you're not going to like whose side we're on."

Before Ben could ask her what she meant, Bobbie ran back to the village wall. Her diamond pickaxe flashed as she began cutting holes in the barrier.

"What are you doing?" Ben cried, grabbing her arm.

"Stopping a bloodbath!" she answered. "We need the Overlords to retreat. It's the only way to end this quickly!"

An arrow whizzed between them. Ben whirled around to see Kyro approaching with an unhinged look in his eyes.

"Traitors in our midst. Spies!" he yelled. "I saw their treachery with my own eyes!"

Ben held up his hands. "Hold on, Kyro," he said. "It's not what it looks like."

"Ha!" said Bobbie, and she cut away more of the wall. "Sound the retreat, Kyro! You can't win this battle!"

Kyro screamed, firing a series of arrows their way. Ben sort of understood where he was coming from—but he didn't want Bobbie to suffer the same fate as the heroes' hole-strewn wall. He pulled her out of Kyro's range, nearly dragging her into the midst of the zombie horde. Their claws would do less damage than Kyro's arrows, Ben reasoned, and soon they'd lost the bard in the chaos.

And the scene was certainly chaotic. Heroes, zombies, and pillagers all fought one another in a confused melee. Arrows flew from all sides, villagers ran about in a blind panic, zombies busted down closed doors, and Bobbie was setting fire to the cafeteria.

Wait a minute. Bobbie was doing what?!

"Bobbie!" Ben cried. "Have you lost your mind?"

"It's the only way," Bobbie said again.

"Bobbie, your *brother* is in that building!"

Ben saw the shock register on Bobbie's face, but he didn't stick around to hear her response. He charged into the burning building, passing tables strewn with food and an entire wall of furnaces. In a back storage room, he found Johnny right where he'd left him. The zombie boy's lead was tied firmly to a post. He'd be completely helpless if the fire spread here.

As Ben removed the post, Bobbie burst into the room. "Johnny!" she cried. "Oh, Johnny, I'm so sorry."

Bobbie rushed to her brother, taking off his pumpkin helmet to get a good look at him before pulling him into an embrace. The zombie boy grumbled and squirmed, but he didn't try to bite through her armor.

Ben figured that's what *family* meant. No matter how much you got on each other's nerves, biting was off-limits.

"Lots of catching up to do, I'm sure," said Ben. "But it's about to get very hot in here."

"We'll go out the back way," Bobbie said, and she cut through the wall with her pickaxe. "Both of you, stick close to me."

As they ran out of the building, Ben leaned in close to Johnny. "Is it me, or is she even bossier than before?"

Johnny growled and swiped at him. Typical. Bobbie almost cooks him, and she gets a hug. And what did Ben get?

Thunk.

Ben got an arrow in the shoulder.

"No!" cried Bobbie. She pulled out her shield and put herself between Ben and his attacker. It was Kyro, eyes burning with fury. When those eyes landed on Johnny—who no longer wore his pumpkin helmet—they bulged in alarm. "Your sidekick is a zombie?! And . . . and . . . nothing rhymes with zombie!"

In the instant before Kyro fired another arrow, a great roar sounded from nearby. The bard flinched, and his shot flew wild.

Ben saw the source of the inhuman noise. A massive, four-legged beast with fearsome horns charged through the hole in the village wall, batting aside two heroes with a single thrust of its great head.

"That's—that's a *ravager*," Ben said through teeth clenched

126

in pain. The building at his back was now a raging inferno. "Bobbie's right, Kyro. The battle is lost. You have to retreat—all of you."

Kyro hesitated, but he clearly saw the truth in what Ben had said. The heroes could handle a raid or a siege, but not both at once.

The bard sent up a flare. It soared into the sky, then exploded in a starburst of radiant light. "Into the hills! We must retreat!" he cried. "Be quick about it now. Beat feet!"

Bobbie evidently saw her chance to slip away. She hurried off while Kyro's back was turned, pulling Johnny and Ben behind her.

But Kyro called after them as they went. "I'll remember you three. Bards never forget. Your actions today . . . are ones you'll regret."

CHAPTER 22

Bobbie could tell right away that Ben was upset. As the burning, broken village disappeared behind them, he was silent.

Ben was many things. But he was so very rarely silent.

"What's wrong?" asked Bobbie. When Ben ignored her and kept running, she grabbed his arm, forcing him to stop—to *look* at her. "Tell me," she said.

Ben frowned. "Fine. I'll tell you what's wrong," he said. And then his eyes went wide, and he said, "As soon as I'm done hallucinating."

Bobbie saw the dim blue glow in the corner of her eye, and she knew what she'd find when she turned around. "Layla, hi!" she said, and she accepted the allay's latest apple. "You missed quite a battle just now."

The allay trilled, then flew off once more. Ben and Johnny both watched her go, transfixed.

"Okay, talk later!" Bobbie shouted after the mob. Then she handed the apple to Ben. "You were injured back there. You should eat."

Ben took the apple, but he wore a look of utter confusion. "What just happened?" he asked.

"That was Layla. She's an allay. I rescued her from the pillager outpost."

Ben's eyebrows rose. "The pillager outpost where you single-handedly defeated a pillager captain."

Bobbie shrugged. "I guess. I mean, I defeated a couple of them, and they weren't wearing name tags. But it was mostly because of lucky shots, and I was just trying to help Benjamin—I mean, Other Ben . . ."

"You were there with Other Ben?" Ben asked, his voice strained.

"No, Other Ben was there with—Phantom!"

Ben was confused. "Phantom? What's that have to do with—"

"Duck!" cried Bobbie, and she pulled him to the ground just as a large, batlike creature rocketed over their crouched bodies. Its glowing eyes were streaks of green as it passed them, and it beat its tattered wings, returning to the sky. Bobbie knew it would soon circle around for another attack.

Johnny leaped forward, snarling. Bobbie had dropped his lead, and he came quickly to her defense, just as he had when phantoms had attacked them on the night that they'd met Ben.

As before, the phantoms were drawn to the group because Bobbie had gone too long without sleep.

Like zombies, phantoms were undead mobs. They only came out at night. And, Bobbie knew, they always hunted in packs. Even if Johnny managed to knock a few of them out of the air, they would soon be overwhelmed.

Ben drew his crossbow. "We need—"

"Shelter," Bobbie finished his thought. She quickly carved a hiding hollow in the side of a small cliff. "This is safer than digging down," she explained.

Johnny followed her into the hollow. Ben went last, plugging the entrance with dirt behind him. If he expected darkness, he was going to be surprised. Bobbie had already set out torches. She went to work expanding the space, cutting away more stone.

"Sorry about that," she said. "I haven't slept in . . . I don't know how long. Being underground really messes with your sense of time, you know?"

"What does it do to your sense of morality?" Ben asked.

Bobbie stopped digging. "What's *that* supposed to mean?"

"Those were people's homes back there, Bobbie. You set them on fire!"

"I set the *cafeteria* on fire," Bobbie corrected.

"You tore down their wall. You let the monsters in. You basically did to that village what Logan did to yours!"

Bobbie felt her cheeks grow hot. "That isn't a fair comparison," she said. "If I helped destroy that village, I did it to save the people who lived there . . . and the zombie villagers that those so-called heroes would have hurt without a second thought." She shook her head sadly. "I didn't see any other solutions. And I didn't hear any ideas at all from *you*."

Bobbie could see her words had hurt Ben, and she felt immediately guilty. When Ben and Logan had been together, Logan had treated Ben like he was worthless. It wasn't true, but Bobbie's words might have made Ben feel worthless all over again. "Ben, I'm sorry. I didn't mean that. And you know there's nobody I'd rather have next to me in a fight."

Johnny growled, and Bobbie laughed. "Okay, well, it's a tie, then!"

Ben didn't join in when she laughed. "Do you even *need* help in a fight?" he asked sullenly.

"What do you mean?"

"I was with the Overlords before the attack, trying to convince them that they needed to evacuate the village. But when I learned they'd sent you into a dangerous situation, I rushed underground to save you." Ben shook his head. "You didn't need saving. We were only apart for a little while, and in that time, you raided outposts, befriended an allay, and became this . . . this hypercompetent fighter. While I've done nothing but babysit. And I didn't even do that very well."

"I'll bet that's not true," said Bobbie. "I know more than anybody that Johnny's a handful. I wouldn't have trusted him with anybody else. Not anybody else in the whole Overworld, Ben. And look!" Bobbie patted her brother's matted hair. "He's safe.

He's healthy. Or . . . not. Whatever the equivalent is for the undead. You kept him safe. You proved I was right to have faith in
you."

Ben's face showed the very beginnings of a small smile. "I
mean, I did save him from a pirate."

"I knew it!" said Bobbie. "You've had all sorts of adventures
together."

"Oh!" said Ben. "And I almost forgot about the rotting humanoid pig beast. We barely escaped that one."

Bobbie laughed again. "I know you're making that up to
scare me, and it isn't working."

Johnny growled.

"You know, Ben," Bobbie said, serious now, "I didn't know
how to do any of this stuff before I met you. I never would have
survived out here without your lessons."

Ben crossed his arms. "Well, good. But I've got one more lesson for you: We're a team. We need to see this through to the
end—together. No more leaving teammates behind."

"Tell that to Layla," said Bobbie. "She keeps disappearing
when I need backup!"

"I'm serious, Bobbie," Ben said, and Johnny growled as he
said it, adding a bit of gravitas.

"You're right," Bobbie said. "I'm sorry that I left you—both of
you. It wasn't right for me to make that choice for you."

Ben turned toward Johnny. "What do you think?" he asked.
"Do we forgive her?"

Johnny gnawed on his bone, evidently bored by all the talking.

Ben shrugged. "Okay. All is forgiven."

"And no more leaving teammates behind," said Bobbie.

They shook on it, and Ben felt a flare of pain where Kyro's arrow had struck him. "Ouch," he said. "Hey, uh . . . you got any more of those apples?"

Bobbie laughed. "So many apples," she said.

CHAPTER 23

"So what do you know about Pigstep Peggy?" Bobbie asked.

Ben, Bobbie, and Johnny were approaching the summit of a mountain. They felt an urgency to keep moving. They didn't want to waste the head start they had on Logan. But they also had to make their way carefully up the steep incline, stopping to place dirt blocks whenever they found no place to put their feet. And Johnny, in his overlarge pumpkin helmet once more, was slightly unsteady on his feet. It was slow going, and with the sun out and no hostile mobs in sight . . . and Bobbie at his side . . . Ben felt more relaxed than he had in ages.

This is what he loved more than anything: exploring a new area with his friends. Literally anything could be on the other side of this mountain!

"Hello? Ben?" said Bobbie. "Pigstep Peggy?"

"Oh, sorry," said Ben, and he reined in his wandering mind.

"I don't know much of anything, really, except that she's next on the list of Logan's targets." He shook his head. "She must have done something to anger him."

"Or embarrass him," said Bobbie. "The boy does not deal with rejection well."

"Who does?" Ben said lightly. "At least he wrote down coordinates for his targets, so we know where to go." Ben placed a dirt block, testing it with his foot before using it as a bridge. "Anyway, I asked Kyro about Peggy. This was *before* you destroyed his home and he turned against us with the fury of a cornered enderman."

"Too soon to joke about it," Bobbie singsonged.

"And Kyro said that she's this big-deal adventurer from back in the day. *Way* back in the day. All of the Overlords look up to her, but her adventuring days are long over. She keeps to herself."

"So Logan is leading an army of zombies to destroy a reclusive, retired grandma type?" Bobbie scoffed. "That's a new low, even for him."

"And we're about to reach new heights!" said Ben. "The summit is just ahead."

"Finally," said Bobbie. "Next time, we cut through the mountain."

"That diamond pickaxe isn't going to last forever," Ben warned.

They were quiet as they crested the peak. Ben expected to see a great expanse of greenery spread out below them. He expected Pigstep Peggy's home to be a little dot nestled among fields of flowers.

That's not what they saw.

"It's a volcano," Ben whispered as he peered over the edge at the lava far below. "It's a volcano with a *building* inside it."

"That can't be what we're looking for," said Bobbie.

Ben checked the map. "The coordinates are right. That's where Logan expects to find Pigstep Peggy."

"But . . . but I was expecting a cozy grandma cottage," said Bobbie. "Not a haunted death fortress suspended above a roiling pit of lava."

"It is a little intimidating, isn't it?" Ben said lightly. Although the sun was up above, pouring sunlight directly into the volcano, the structure was so dark that it almost seemed to swallow the light. "It's not too late to turn back."

Bobbie sighed. "It kind of *is* too late, though. Come on." She grabbed his hand, pulling him over the rim of the volcano as purposefully as she pulled Johnny on his lead. "We're gonna save this sweet old lady if it's the last thing we do."

Ben groaned. The last thing they did? He wished Bobbie wouldn't tempt fate like that.

The squat black fortress grew more frightening the closer they got to it. It crouched in the volcano like a great spider, with tiny stone walkways suspended above the lava like webbing. The way down was steep, and more than once Ben fought off waves of vertigo. It was a treacherous descent that forced them to crouch as they moved slowly forward. And the longer it took, the more time Ben had to doubt the entire endeavor.

At length, they made it to a simple stone platform that hugged the inside of the volcano. They were on the same level as the fortress, but to reach it, they would have to walk one of the narrow stone pathways that hovered above the lava.

"Don't look down," Bobbie warned.

"Right," said Ben. "Because looking straight ahead at the death castle is *so* reassuring."

The pathway was only one block wide, so they had to go single file. Ben walked in front—not because he felt brave (he didn't), but because Bobbie had Johnny by the lead, and they thought the best place for the zombie boy was in the rear.

Who knew how Pigstep Peggy would react to a zombie crossing the bridge to her home?

For that matter—who knew how she'd react to *people* crossing the bridge? She hadn't exactly put out a "welcome" sign.

While the bridge itself was stone, Ben could see, by the time they were midway across it, that the black material of the fort was obsidian. He'd suspected that from a distance, but it was hard to believe. A fortress made of obsidian would be tremendously secure. And the place was *huge*, with multiple towers looming above them. It looked almost like a dark, twisted vision of a city.

"The obsidian," said Bobbie. "It looks like it's . . . *wet*. Like it's dripping with violet."

"Oh, wow. It's *weeping* obsidian," Ben said, with more than a little awe in his voice. Now that she'd pointed it out, he could see the telltale rivulets of violet streaming off the otherwise solid-black blocks. "That stuff is super rare. Pigstep Peggy must have been adventuring for *years* to get her hands on this much of it."

"That's bad news," said Bobbie, "if our plan is to get her to leave. She's invested a lot into this build."

"Or maybe she's ready to get back to adventuring?" Ben shrugged. "She could be the third member of our party."

Johnny didn't even have to groan at that. Bobbie did it for him.

"Fourth member," Ben corrected himself. "Because the mindless undead toddler definitely counts."

"Of course he does," said Bobbie. "After all, he's second-in-command."

"Second-in . . . ?" said Ben.

"And don't forget Layla," said Bobbie. "She's been so helpful. We might never have to scrounge for food again. I'd say she's the MVP of our little adventuring party."

"Hold on, I'm still the leader, though, right?" At Bobbie's silent smile, he said again, "Right?"

It was at that moment that Ben's foot came down on a pressure plate.

Ben froze immediately, and he signaled for Bobbie and Johnny to stop, too. The pressure plate was well hidden, but he recognized the subtle shift and the familiar click.

"What is it?"

"Booby trap," he answered. Ben began to sweat. What would happen when he lifted his foot? Would the bridge collapse beneath them? Would an explosion knock them off the narrow path and into the lake of lava below?

"Off the path," he said. "Build to the side — get some distance between us."

Bobbie reluctantly began to lay dirt beside the bridge, build-ing a sort of detour from the path. "What about you?" she asked.

"If I'm blasted into the air . . . try to catch me," Ben answered.

He held his breath.

"Ben, wait—" said Bobbie.

He braced himself.

"Groar!" said Johnny.

He lifted his foot.

Nothing happened.

"What was it?" Ben asked, crouching low, not quite trusting that something wasn't about to explode.

"There," said Bobbie, and she pointed in the direction of the obsidian structure. "There was a red light. It turned off when you moved your foot."

Ben put his foot back down on the switch. He saw the red light illuminate one of the structure's windows. When he lifted his foot, the light turned off again.

"It's a redstone torch," said Ben.

Bobbie scratched her head. "But why . . . ?"

"It's a signal," said Ben. "An *alarm*." He turned to Bobbie. "I hope Pigstep Peggy is friendly. Because she knows we're coming now." He shook his head. "And the weeping fortress tucked away in a volcano and surrounded by lava and wired with an alarm sort of gives me the impression she's not excited about uninvited guests."

CHAPTER 24

Alerted to the possibility of booby traps, Bobbie decided not to return to the narrow stone bridge. Instead she used up her inventory of dirt blocks to create a parallel path. Johnny followed close behind, with Ben now bringing up the rear.

As they drew closer, the weeping of the obsidian blocks became more obvious . . . and more eerie. It gave the entire fortress an otherworldly quality. It was almost as if the place were alive. Alive . . . and full of sorrow.

The various bridges crisscrossing the lava all met in a small patch of stone at the base of the fortress. Peggy's "front yard" was barren and gray, just a featureless cobblestone courtyard set before a purplish red door.

As the door creaked open, Bobbie and Ben stood suddenly at

attention. Bobbie pulled out her shield. She had no idea what to expect.

But the old woman who appeared in the open doorway didn't seem at all threatening.

Pigstep Peggy was a gray-haired woman with a craggy smile. She didn't look like an adventurer. In fact, Bobbie noticed that she dressed much like a farmer, with brown coveralls and a wide-brimmed, woven hat. If she had weapons on her, they were stashed away in her inventory where Bobbie couldn't see them.

In short, despite the tremendously imposing black-and-purple structure that loomed above their heads, and the lava bubbling ominously below them, Bobbie felt immediately at ease when she laid eyes on Peggy. Finally, here was someone who didn't seem to be spoiling for a fight.

"Hello, my dears," said Peggy. "A long way from the path, aren't you? You must be lost."

"I don't think so," said Ben. "We're looking for Pigstep Peggy. That's you, right?"

Her eyes narrowed. "Where did you hear that name?"

Bobbie stepped forward, putting herself between them. "We heard stories about a great adventurer—a *hero*—and we were hoping to meet her."

"I'm sorry to disappoint you," said Peggy. "But I'm just an old woman, and I value my privacy. So if you don't mind—"

Bobbie opened her mouth to protest—at the very least, this woman needed to be warned about Logan—when, suddenly, a flash of blue appeared in her peripheral vision. Layla cooed, extending an apple.

"Well, look at that," said Peggy. "I've seen a lot in my day, but *that* is something new." She opened the door wider to give Bobbie and Ben a closer look and—for the first time—her eyes landed on Johnny. "That's new, too! Who's that in the pumpkin? Have you taken a *zombie* as a pet?"

"Not a pet," answered Bobbie. "A brother."

The woman seemed confused by that. She looked from Bobbie to Johnny and back again. "Is that so?" the woman said, and Bobbie wondered what she found more confusing: that Bobbie's brother was a *zombie* or a *villager*. After a moment, she tutted. "Well, you must come in and tell me all about it. But call me Peg—I'm afraid my pigstepping days are behind me. Old joints, you know."

Bobbie flashed a smile at Ben. This was the warmest welcome they'd had since their travels had begun.

But Ben appeared confused. "Pigstepping. What does that even mean?"

"You don't know how to pigstep, eh?" Peg grinned. "Seems I might have a thing or two to teach you after all."

The interior of Peg's home was as cozy as the exterior was fearsome. The weeping obsidian was only the outermost layer—inside, the walls were made of vibrant dark wood that was brightened with plentiful artworks, and the windows let in a great deal of light. Bobbie realized that the lava would provide lighting, even in the dead of night. Glittering crystals of a type Bobbie didn't recognize adorned nearly every surface.

Peg noticed Bobbie's interest. "Pretty, isn't it, dear? That's quartz. I've quite a fondness for it."

"Quartz—crafted from nether quartz ore, I bet," said Ben. "Plus weeping obsidian. And is that an Ender pearl on the book-shelf?" Ben whistled, impressed. "I'm sensing a theme."

"What?" asked Bobbie. "I don't know what you mean."

Ben turned toward their host. "I'm guessing Peg has spent time in the Nether."

Peg chuckled. "Quite a lot of time," she said. Bobbie thought it sounded almost wistful, as if Peg wished she were in the Nether at that very moment.

"I've heard of it," said Bobbie. "It's another dimension, right?"

"Even I've never been there," said Ben. "Logan told me I wouldn't last five minutes."

Logan. Hearing the name reminded Bobbie of the urgency of their mission. Logan might already be on his way here.

"The Nether is a strange place," said Peg. "Wild! And dangerous. But like any place, there are rules. Patterns. Once you know them, it's not so strange. Not so very dangerous."

"I'd love to hear all about it," said Bobbie. "But there's a reason we're here. We came to warn you."

"Warn me, dear?" said Peg. "Whatever about?"

"An army of the undead," answered Bobbie. "They're being led this way by a bitter bully named Logan."

"Oh, my," said Peg.

"The Overworld Overlords have already fallen," Ben added. "Their home was destroyed, and their team was scattered."

"Oh, my! How sad for them." Peg shook her head. "Always a pity when young people get in over their heads. But you don't need to worry about me, dears. Old Peg can take care of herself."

Ben and Bobbie shared a look. Peg wasn't taking this nearly seriously enough.

In the silence, they heard a muffled sound coming from nearby.

"What was that?" asked Bobbie.

"What was what?" Peg said lightly.

"It was coming from that door," said Ben. "Is someone else here?"

"That door leads to my cellar," Peg said, not answering the question.

"Logan might be here already," said Bobbie. "He travels underground with his army. What if they're coming up through the basement?"

"It did sound sort of like a zombie," said Ben.

"Pish posh," said Peg. "You probably heard your brother over there, grunting through his pumpkin head. And you still haven't told me *that* story." Peg led Ben and Bobbie to a table and chairs—in the opposite direction from the cellar door. "Peg has alarms and traps aplenty, and that weeping obsidian isn't just for looks, you know—it's plenty sturdy enough to keep out unwanted guests. So relax! Make yourselves comfortable, dears, while I put on some stew. How do you like mushrooms? Your Peg is a vegetarian, did you know?"

Bobbie thought better of arguing with their host.

But Johnny, left behind in the front room, never took his eyes off that cellar door.

CHAPTER 25

eg invited them to spend the night. Bobbie agreed happily, but Ben was reluctant. "There's something off about her," he whispered when Peg's back was turned.

"Ben, please," whispered Bobbie. "I haven't slept in a week. I've been spending my nights in underground hidey-holes, a few blocks away from a horde of the undead. If there's an extra bed here, I want it."

Ben found he couldn't argue with that. It had been some time since he'd slept, too. And they clearly needed more time to convince Peg that Logan was a real threat to her.

"Is it possible you've met Logan?" he asked her. "He attacked the Overlords because they wouldn't let him join them. Does he have some personal vendetta against you?"

"Oh, anything's possible," said Peg, smiling with quiet amusement. "One does make enemies in the hero business. But I tried not to leave any of *mine* alive. Cake?"

Peg held out a freshly baked cake.

"Uh, I'm good," said Ben.

Bobbie shrugged. "I'll have some cake."

"That a girl," said Peg, and she took a seat across from them. "Now, I do tend to get young adventurers dropping in on me from time to time. They ask to apprentice with me; they want me to train them or give them some special insight into the adventurer's life." Peg shook her head. "I turn them away, every one. I'm not looking for a sidekick."

Ben looked over at Bobbie, who nodded. "That fits," Ben said. "Logan wants to punish everyone who ever rejected him. You must have turned him down at some point."

"Congratulations on being an *excellent* judge of character," said Bobbie.

"It's clear *you two* have some things you could teach *me*," said Peg. "How do you keep the zombie from attacking you?"

Ben didn't really like how she called Johnny *the zombie*. "Bobbie told you already. Johnny's her brother."

"You meant that literally, then?" said Peg. "But that only piques my curiosity all the more."

"The short answer is, it took a lot of training," said Bobbie, with a mouth full of cake. "And he still sometimes tries to attack if he's overstimulated. He hates the helmet, but it keeps him from biting. He also likes gnawing on a bone."

"Charming," said Peg. And it was subtle, but Ben was certain he saw her eyes drift back to the cellar door.

And he heard a low, rumbling sound.

"What was that?" Ben asked.

"Oh my!" said Peggy, and she put her hands to her stomach. "I guess I shouldn't have eaten all that cake. Your Peg has a hard time with gluten, if I didn't mention it."

Ben narrowed his eyes with suspicion. "I didn't notice you eating any of the cake."

"Anyway, it's getting late," said Peg, and when Ben began to protest, she added, "Us old folk need to turn in early, and I'll ask you to respect that. Come on, I'll show you to your rooms."

"If you're sure," Ben said to Bobbie.

"I'm sure," said Bobbie. "Then we can talk more about Logan in the morning. Maybe formulate a plan."

"Whatever you say, dear," said Peg, and she picked up a nearby lantern. "I'm sure everything will seem less dire in the morning."

Ben was shown to a tiny guest room—nothing but a bed, a chest, and a stone furnace, with a one-block window set too high to provide a good view. Logan might have been a top-tier jerk, but at least *his* creepy castle had included comfortable bedrooms.

Not that Ben was in the mood to get comfortable. Bobbie may have fallen for Pigstep Peggy's kindly grandmother routine, but Ben wasn't buying it. Not for a second.

Through the tiny window, Ben could see a bit of sky, just past the rim of the volcano. When the moon passed by, he would know it was the middle of the night. He'd wait until then before he enacted his plan.

He hoped Peggy was a heavy sleeper.

CHAPTER 26

obbie awoke with the feeling that something was wrong. It was still night—a beam of moonlight shone in from the bedroom's single small window. So much for a full night's sleep. Bobbie tried to clear the fog from her mind. What was wrong? Why had she startled awake?

The answers came to her in a rush: Johnny was missing.

And Pigstep Peg was sitting at the foot of her bed.

Bobbie sat up quickly. "Where's Johnny?" she asked. "What happened?"

"Calm yourself, dear," said Peg. "I've brought you some milk and cookies."

Bobbie's mind felt slow to wake. "What? I don't want cookies. Did Johnny get out? Is he all right?"

"Johnny is quite safe. I promise." Peg chuckled. "That carved pumpkin does make him easier to manage, doesn't it? I was able to handle him without a great deal of fuss."

"You didn't hurt him?" said Bobbie. "If you did—"

"I told you, he's safe. But you love him, don't you? As a big sister should. That's very good." Peg smiled, nodded. "Ben will take care of him. You trust Ben, isn't that right?"

"You took Johnny to Ben's room? Why?"

"Well, that's because I need your help, dear. And where we're going, your brother might not be safe. Not like he is with your Ben." Peg gestured for Bobbie to stand. "Up now. Up and at 'em. We've got an adventure to go on, but we'll be back before you know it."

Bobbie rose warily to her feet. "I thought you didn't want a sidekick."

"I don't," said Peg. "But an adventurer who can tame zombies and befriend blue spirits? You're something special, dear. And any adventurer will tell you . . ." Peg leaned in close. "Always use the right tool for the job."

Peg led Bobbie down the winding paths of her fortress. It felt even bigger on the inside than on the outside. Within seconds, Bobbie was completely turned around. She wouldn't have been able to find Ben's room now if she tried.

"If this is about an adventure, we should really get Ben. I'm new to all this. Ben taught me everything I know about combat."

Peg clucked her tongue. "It isn't combat I need help with. And adventurers like Ben are an emerald a dozen. If you met those hoity-toity Overlords, you know that's the truth."

"Ben's different," Bobbie said quickly. "But . . . I know what you mean about the Overlords and adventurers like them. I grew up in a village, and adventurers would storm through and take whatever they wanted. They treated my friends and neighbors like they didn't matter."

"All in the pursuit of glory and gold, experience and excitement!" Peg nodded. "I know the type. I was a . . . different sort of adventurer. I wanted to understand the world. I wanted to forge connections. So, no, I'm not asking for your help fighting. It's your *noncombat* skills I'm hoping will be of help. Ah! Here we are."

Peg turned a corner, and the hallway opened up into a tall-ceilinged chamber lined with armor stands, crafting stations, and chests. It looked like a war room, and at its center was a single structure. Although it wasn't activated, Bobbie immediately recognized the upright black ring for what it was.

"A Nether portal," breathed Bobbie.

"That's right," said Peg. "Let's find you some new armor, shall we? The Nether is hot this time of year . . ." Peg grinned darkly. "And of course, it can be very, very dangerous."

Bobbie knew that already. Everything she'd heard of the Nether made it sound like a perilous hellscape. But at least Peg had a lot of firsthand experience.

Peg outfitted her with a dark gray chest plate, a golden helm, and iron boots that appeared almost purple in the lantern light.

Peg herself wore gold from head to toe. "Nice look, isn't it?" she asked. "For a while, I used to call myself Gold-Plated Peg. But of course 'Pigstep Peggy' is the name that stuck!"

"What about weapons?" asked Bobbie.

"Bring whatever you like. But I'll do my best to keep us out of any combat situations." Peg tutted and shook her head. "When you get to be my age, you begin to find violence somewhat distasteful."

"I agree with you in theory," said Bobbie. "But if this sword is up for grabs, I'm not going to turn it down."

"Good eye! That's the best sword I've got," said Peg. "You've got an inner fire to you, girl. You may just fit right in, where we're going. Oh, and speaking of fire . . ."

Peg produced a flint and steel. Holding them near the inert portal, she struck them together, producing a spark—a spark that flared into a flame, a flame that activated the portal, which ignited in a burst of glittering purple light. Even knowing the danger it represented, Bobbie thought it was beautiful.

Peg seemed to know just what she was thinking. "Pretty, right?" she said. "Don't trust it. That pretty purple light has lured many an adventurer to their doom."

Bobbie leaned in closer. The portal shimmered like a ghostly gem—or like the surface of the sea, which Bobbie had only recently seen for the first time. Her world had been so small, before the zombie siege changed everything. Since then, she'd seen a dozen biomes, traveled from one end of the Overworld to the other. And now—would she travel *beyond* the Overworld?

Peg giggled like a little girl. "Go on, dear. After you!"

And then the woman gently but firmly pushed her forward, face-first into that shimmering purple sheen. Bobbie closed her eyes.

She opened them on a whole new world.

CHAPTER 27

When the moon rose above the volcano, Ben enacted his plan.

It wasn't a very involved one. But Ben had found that the best plans tended to be simple.

Step one: Sneak out of his room.

Step two: Think about finding Bobbie and waking her up.

Step three: Remember that Bobbie had been exhausted, and Johnny would be with her, and Johnny was *not* suited to stealth missions.

Step four: Decide to do this one on his own.

Peg's fort was big, and its twisting hallways seemed almost purposely disorienting. But Ben had spent enough time digging around underground to develop a keen sense of direction, even without the benefit of moon, sun, or compass. He retraced the steps he had taken with Peg when she'd led him to his room.

He found the staircase to the ground floor and, peeking around the corner, found the little kitchen area empty. There were no torches or lanterns lit, but the orange glow of the lava streamed in through the windows, providing enough light to see by.

Still, it was dim enough to be eerie. And there was something sinister—even villainous—about relying on lava for lighting. Ben found that he simply didn't trust Peg. Maybe Bobbie's hero skepticism was rubbing off on him. The Overworld Overlords hadn't exactly lived up to his expectations, and Logan, of course, had been a tremendous disappointment. Why should he expect Peggy to be any different?

There was an easy way to learn whether Peg was trustworthy: snooping. In particular, Ben felt he needed to know what Peg was hiding in her basement. It sounded like something was *alive* down there. Did she have a prisoner? What if Logan had already attacked, and Peg had won? It would explain why she was so unconcerned.

Or maybe she kept a cow down there for milk and sheep for wool? A little indoor farm, safely tucked away from the lava and the arid, rocky platform that passed for a lawn. Ben wasn't certain that the basement's secret was a sinister one. But he knew she kept *something* down there, away from prying eyes.

Whatever she was hiding, Ben would know soon enough. He crept through the simple kitchen and into the entrance hall, where the nether quartz glittered in the lava glow. There he saw the lone door that led to the basement.

Ben was determined to be stealthy. He reminded himself not to make a sound.

But when Ben opened that cellar door . . . when he saw Pig-step Peggy's horrible secret for himself . . . all his plans were forgotten.

Ben opened his mouth, and he screamed.

CHAPTER 28

obbie had heard stories about the Nether. Back in Plain-town, when adventurers would pass through between quests, they liked to talk—and they *loved* to brag. The places they'd been, the monsters they'd vanquished, the dangers they'd overcome.

Many of the greatest of those dangers called the Nether home. Living columns of flame and smoke, jumping lumps of sentient magma, and massive monstrosities that adventurers described as "floating baby heads but with tendrils." And beyond all that, the landscape itself was said to be dreadful, with cascading rivers of lava, resource-starved deserts, and an oppressive ceiling of rock devoid of sun, moon, or stars.

Bobbie was surprised, therefore, to find lush grass at her feet.

She took a few faltering steps from the portal. The grass was a strange hue of blue, as were the trees that grew all around the portal. Only they weren't trees, Bobbie realized, but enormous fungi. Mushrooms! It was like something out of a storybook. Great vines reached into the sky, and although there was lava, it wasn't as fearsome as she'd imagined. Glowing orange against the dark sky, the distant lavafalls took her breath away.

"Not what you were expecting?" Peg said at her back.

"I'd always heard it was an infernal nightmare. 'A plane of ravenous fire and death.' That's a direct quote."

"It *is* those things," said Peg. "But it's other things, too. There are forests here, if strange ones, and entire civilizations unlike any you've seen before. Here's an important lesson: Life finds a way to thrive in even the most unforgiving biome."

Bobbie liked that. She liked this. Learning from Peg felt altogether different from Ben's lessons. Since meeting Ben, Bobbie had been in a constant struggle to survive—and to keep her brother safe. Here, with Peg, everything felt strangely calm—as if the woman had seen it all and had gained a quiet self-assurance. Her confidence radiated from her very being. It was contagious.

Peg seemed to read something in Bobbie's face, and she nodded with approval. "It's always good to meet a young person who is open to words of wisdom. Your parents must be exceptional people."

Bobbie nodded somberly. "They were. They are! They're . . . currently zombies. But I'm working on that."

Peg looked confused, which Bobbie supposed was a natural enough reaction. "I've never heard of adventurers becoming zombies," she said. "I've heard of adventurers getting *eaten* by zombies, of course. But not transforming."

"Oh," said Bobbie. "My parents aren't adventurers. They're actually villagers."

Peg's confusion deepened.

"I'm adopted," Bobbie explained.

"How curious," said Peg.

"My parents are part of the horde that's marching this way," said Bobbie. "That's . . . sort of the real reason we're here. Not just to warn you, but to ask you not to hurt the zombies."

"My bastion can withstand a zombie siege, dear. You needn't worry about old Peg. I'm content to sit by the cozy fire and ignore the zombies entirely. This Logan nuisance will give up eventually, I'm sure."

"That . . . maybe that could work," Bobbie said. And the more she thought about it, the more hopeful she became. If Peg could hold off the horde, it could buy Bobbie time to assemble the cures she needed.

"I wouldn't recommend daydreaming, dearie. This forest is *teeming* with endermen. You don't want to lock eyes with one by accident."

Bobbie cast her eyes to the ground. As Peg's gold-plated feet moved at a brisk pace, she hurried to keep up. The Nether might have been more beautiful than she'd expected, but that didn't mean Bobbie wanted to be alone there.

After a short hike, Peg stepped to the edge of a cliff. She motioned for Bobbie to join her. As Bobbie stepped forward, the fungal trees parted, allowing her an unobstructed view of the landscape. She saw a great lake of lava and an eerie gray desert; dark figures moved across its monotone surface. In the distance, massive jellyfish-like creatures drifted aimlessly against the black sky, tendrils trailing below them.

And dead ahead, there was a crumbling fortress made of black stone. Bobbie couldn't shake the feeling she'd seen the structure before, and recently. "Is that—your fortress?"

Peg nodded. "Good eye. I modeled my home after this place. It's what's left of a bastion. It's old and crumbling, but you can imagine how magnificent it would have been when it was new. It's still magnificent, really—but my own version is built of sturdier stuff."

Peg began the descent, following a narrow path that wound its way down the sheer cliff face. Bobbie couldn't tell whether the trail was natural or Peg had carved these steps with her pickaxe, but either way, the retired adventurer clearly knew the path well. She was as certain of her footing as a mountain goat, whereas Bobbie took great care with each step.

"Come on now," said Peg. "Pick up the pace! We'll skirt the edge of the soul sand valley and make our way to the bastion remnant. I'm eager to introduce you to my friends."

Bobbie was surprised by that. "You have friends? Here, in the Nether?"

"I most certainly do," answered Peg. "And they'll be your friends, too . . . so long as you keep that gold helmet of yours on."

That was fine with Bobbie. She certainly didn't want to have *less* armor . . . not as she followed Pigstep Peggy into the crumbling remains of a once-great fortress.

CHAPTER 29

Peg walked the empty corridors with quiet confidence. Bobbie tried to mimic her boldness, but she felt an icy thread of fear in her stomach. The bastion felt haunted somehow. She could sense its history—and she was sure it was a history of violence and sorrow.

Peg seemed to come alive, though. Gone was the old woman who tottered around her kitchen preparing cake and talking about her old joints. In her place was an adventurer—one who walked with a spring in her step.

She came to a stop in an open courtyard. "Quiet, isn't it?"

"Did someone used to live here?" Bobbie asked. "What happened to them?"

"Oh, did you think this place was deserted? Far from it," said Peg. "They've had us surrounded since we crossed the bridge."

"What?!" said Bobbie. "Who is *they*?"

"I forgot how shy they are around new people. Here." Peg slipped Bobbie a gold ingot. "Hold that out and make pig noises."

"Pig noises?" said Bobbie. "Like . . . oink oink?"

"Good enough," said Peg, and she inclined her head toward the edge of the courtyard. Deep shadows ringed the area, and as Bobbie looked, she saw movement within them. She and Peg *were* being watched, and the watchers crept forward now, stepping into the light. Bobbie gasped. The beings were humanoid, but they had the features of a pig, with floppy ears, stubby snouts, and small white tusks. Their pink-hued skin glistened in the lava light—and so did their golden swords.

"Ah-ah-ah," warned Peg, when Bobbie took an involuntary step backward. "A piglin won't hurt you, so long as you're wearing gold. And if you give them that ingot, they'll know you're a friend."

Bobbie wasn't sure. The piglins weren't attacking—not yet— but they were fearsome, with their inhuman features and brawny bodies. And, in Bobbie's experience, most mobs didn't carry a sword around unless they were prepared to use it.

She tossed the ingot onto the ground, and the nearest piglin darted forward to retrieve it. As it backed away, it threw something onto the ground where the ingot had been. Bobbie flinched, expecting an attack. But the piglin was only making a trade. Gifting her some item in exchange for the ingot.

Bobbie stepped forward to retrieve the small, luminous green orb.

"Well!" said Peg. "That's an Ender pearl. It's valuable. Shane there must really like you."

"Shane?"

Peg nodded. "I have names for all of them. That's Shane, and Madison, and the one in back is Troy."

Bobbie took another look at the gathered piglins. To her eye, they all looked nearly identical. "Have you . . . spent a lot of time with them?"

Peg chuckled. "You could say that. I lived among these gentle beings for years. I joined their hunting parties, guarded their treasure room from invaders, even cleaned out their hoglin stables. Even with all my years as an adventurer, I never would have survived here without their expertise. Or their art!"

Bobbie took another look at her surroundings. The bastion remnant wasn't just crumbling, it was spartan, with no decorations to speak of—artworks or otherwise. "What kind of art do piglins make?"

"The art of movement," said Peg. "The art . . . of dance!"

With that, the old adventurer raised her arms out at her sides. She moved her arms up and down in a rhythmic motion, and at the same time, she repeatedly bobbed her head. To Bobbie's amazement, the piglins joined in, performing the same series of movements. There was no mistaking it—they were dancing.

Peg laughed joyously, and suddenly the adventurer's nickname made sense to Bobbie. *This* must be pigstepping.

"Oh, I wish I could stay here forever," said Peg as she ended her dance and leaned against a crumbling wall, breathing heavily. "But the Nether isn't meant for human habitation. It's impossible to sleep here, and food is scarce." Peg shook her head. "I visited frequently, as I said, but eventually, I always had to return home. And then, one day . . . I wondered if maybe I could bring a little bit of the Nether back home with me."

As Bobbie watched, Peg extended another gold ingot. "Shane? Come on, buddy. Want the shiny?"

Peg began walking back the way they'd come. She kept the ingot extended as she walked, and Shane followed the gold, like a cow follows wheat.

Bobbie followed, too, and in a few short minutes, they'd made it back to the forest portal.

"After you," Peg said to Bobbie.

Bobbie took a final look at her strange surroundings, then she stepped through the shimmering violet air. The blueish forest around her seemed to warp and waver.

And then, in the blink of an eye, she was back in Peg's castle. She could see now how the adventurer had taken inspiration from the bastion remnant. This structure was what the bastion might have looked like *before* it was a broken remnant.

The portal rippled, and Peg stepped through. There was an unmistakable look of dread on her face.

"What's wrong?" asked Bobbie. "Did something happen to Shane?"

"Something's about to," Peg said with a sober note in her voice. "Watch."

Bobbie *did* watch. She watched as the happy piglin appeared in a wave of violet light.

She watched as the piglin bent over as if in pain. She watched as its body began to shake uncontrollably.

And she watched as Shane transformed, the vibrant pink skin

sloughing off half Shane's face. The piglin was gone . . . replaced by a monster.

A scream rang out, and at first, Bobbie thought it was coming from her own mouth.

But then she recognized the scream. She'd heard it many times before.

"Ben?" she said.

Peg scowled. "What's that fool gotten himself into?"

Bobbie took one more look at the undead horror that the piglin had become—and then she ran out of the room and into the dark heart of Peg's castle.

CHAPTER 30

en stumbled backward, desperate to put space between himself and the horrors of the cellar.

But in his haste, he left the door wide open. And now the horrors of the cellar were climbing out.

"Ben? Are you okay?"

Bobbie came rushing into the room and to Ben's side. As she helped him to his feet, he kept his eyes on the open, pitch-dark doorway.

"M-monsters!" he said, pointing.

As he said it, a creature stepped over the threshold to the cellar and into the central room. It was an undead pig-human hybrid—just like the one that had chased him out of Logan's fortress.

"It's a zombified piglin," Bobbie said flatly. She did not sound nearly panicked enough to Ben's ear.

"Zombified piglins," Ben said. "Plural!"

A second creature crossed the threshold, and a third.

"How many of them are down there?" Bobbie asked, and she took a step toward the doorway. Ben held her back, and she looked to Peg for guidance.

"They aren't hostile," Peg said.

"Sometimes they are," Ben corrected her. "I was once locked in a room with one. It was a fight to the death."

Bobbie gave him a funny look. "How did that happen?" But then the answer dawned on her. "Wait, don't tell me. Logan? Another one of his lessons?"

During their time together, Logan had enjoyed putting Ben into difficult situations. He was still terrified of spiders after Logan had left him to languish in a web.

"Logan," Ben confirmed. "He told me I would never be ready for the Nether unless I could face monstrous pigs in hand-to-hand combat. He locked me in a room with one of them. It tried to kill me!"

Peg scoffed. "And who attacked first?"

Ben remembered it like it was yesterday. "I mean . . . I attacked first, but . . . but Logan told me that was the key to fighting them. To strike quickly, before they could charge."

"He's a liar," said Peg. "And cruel."

"We know that already," said Bobbie.

"They . . . they really aren't hostile? How is that possible?" asked Ben. "They're so . . . *gruesome.*"

"That's very judgmental," said Peg. "Especially coming from a boy who attacked and destroyed a peaceful creature."

Ben's heart sank, and Bobbie shook loose from his grip, stepping past the piglins to peer through the door and down the staircase. Ben knew what she'd see; he'd seen it himself, only moments ago.

The basement was *full* of zombified piglins. There were hundreds of them!

And, apparently, there was at least one non-piggish zombie as well.

"Johnny!" Bobbie cried. "Get up here right now."

Ben peered over Bobbie's shoulder. Johnny was trying to reclaim his bone, which had been taken by one of the piglins. He growled a wordless complaint.

"You have to learn to share your things, Johnny," Bobbie said. "Now get up here, please and thank you!"

Johnny growled again, but he did as his sister instructed.

"There! See?" said Peg, and Ben screamed again—he hadn't realized she had slipped up behind them.

"That was right in my ear," Bobbie complained.

"I'm a little bit on edge right now!" said Ben.

Bobbie crossed her arms. "If you're so freaked out by the piglins, then why did you let Johnny go down there?"

"Me?" said Ben. "You had him in *your* room."

"Until Peg brought him to your room," said Bobbie.

"Uh, no," said Ben. "That didn't happen." The truth dawned on Ben like a blast of TNT. His mouth dropped open. "Oh, you're kidding me."

"What?" said Bobbie.

"Isn't it obvious?" said Ben. "*Pigstep Peggy* here kidnapped him and threw him in her dungeon." Ben turned his iciest glare onto the woman.

"That can't be true," said Bobbie.

"Oh, 'kidnap' is such a strong word," said Peg. "And so is 'dungeon.' I merely set up a play date between your pet zombie . . . and mine."

"He isn't a pet," Bobbie said. "Peg, you know this. He's my brother."

"And why do you have so many zombified piglins in your not-a-dungeon?" asked Ben.

"She's bringing them over from the Nether," Bobbie answered. "She wants to bring piglins here, but when they cross through the portal . . ."

"They transform," confirmed Peg. "They become zombies as soon as they enter the Overworld."

Bobbie shuddered. "I saw it happen with my own eyes. It was horrible."

"I can believe it," said Ben. "I mean, if *these* guys are the end result, it can't be a pretty process." A nearby piglin snorted wetly, and Ben shuddered, too.

"I've tried everything," Peg said. "I've outfitted them with different kinds of armor. I've doused them with splash potions. I even made one invisible before bringing it through." She shook her head. "Nothing has worked. They go through the transformation every single time I bring one through the portal."

"Then maybe . . . stop . . . doing that?" Ben suggested.

"Your Peg gets so lonely," said the adventurer. "The company of fellow humans has always been . . . an awkward fit. But the pig people of the Nether, they don't judge me. They don't find me strange. As long as I wear gold and join them in a dance from time to time, they accept me as one of their own."

As Peg rounded up the stray piglin zombies and forcefully herded them back to the cellar, Bobbie told her, "Careful! Don't be so rough with them."

Peg smiled. "This is exactly why I need your help," she said, whirling on Bobbie. "Where other people see monsters, you see people. You trained your brother! You somehow reached the humanity buried deep inside him. I have to believe you could do the same thing for my poor piglins. You said bones would help, right? I have bones!"

Peg opened a nearby chest, revealing several neat stacks of bones. There were even creepy, pitch-black skulls mixed in among the white.

"Yikes!" Ben said. "Where did you—? No, never mind. I don't want to know."

"I'm not sure about any of this," said Bobbie. "I trained my brother not to bite me. But the zombie piglins don't seem hostile."

"They aren't hostile, but they aren't intelligent, either," said Peg. "They're lacking that *spark*. The rare piggish wit that makes a piglin unique in all the world." Peg appeared on the verge of despair. "Oh, won't you try? You must try. Name your price. I'll give you anything you want!"

"Anything?" Ben asked, grinning.

Bobbie shot him a dirty look. "Don't tell me you still have emeralds on your mind. We've got bigger problems to worry about."

"Oh, I haven't forgotten," said Ben. "But you've been so worried about Logan, you forgot our top priority . . . is getting our hands on the cure."

Bobbie's eyes went wide. "The cure!"

"The cure?" echoed Peg. "What cure?"

"The cure for zombification," answered Ben. "We found it in a witch's journal. But we haven't been able to find the key ingredient."

"I may have it," Peg said quickly. "Or if not, I'll know how to get it. I've been to the End and back. What is it you need?"

"Not so fast," said Ben. "We cure Johnny *first*. And then we try it on the piglins. Deal?"

"Fine. Deal!" said Peg. "Stop stalling. Now tell me, what do we—"

A sound cut through the bastion, long and loud and unexpected. It was coming from outside, and it took Ben a moment to place it. "Was that . . . a goat horn?"

Bobbie's face dropped. "Oh no," she said. "I've heard that horn before." She rushed to the nearest window, and the others followed. In the predawn light, Ben could make out shapes moving on the far side of the bridge. A lot of shapes.

"We're out of time," said Bobbie. "It's Logan. He's here!"

CHAPTER 31

The Overworld was still and quiet as dawn broke over the landscape—so quiet that Logan's voice could be heard from where he stood among his soldiers on the far side of Peg's bridge.

"Pigstep Peggy!" he bellowed. "Give up! You're outnumbered!"

"For now," Peg said, not bothering to shout—her words were intended for Bobbie and Ben. "But he's not going to have much of an army when the sun peeks over the mountain, is he?"

"Normally, you'd be right," said Bobbie. "But take a closer look . . ."

The sun cast its light across the valley, shining upon Logan's forces. Iron helmets glinted in the glare, and not a single zombie burst into flames. Logan had outfitted his army well.

"Well, the boy certainly thinks big," said Peg. "He's got those things in armor? That must have taken an *awful* lot of iron."

"That's what we've been trying to tell you," said Bobbie. "Logan's a serious threat, and he's dead-set on taking you down."

"He's welcome to try," said Peg. "I won't abandon my home." She shrugged. "But I don't mind if it gets a little messy."

Peg slammed a button on the wall, and, with no warning whatsoever, the bridge exploded.

Bobbie looked away, shielding herself from the sudden violence. The bridge had been booby-trapped with TNT—a *lot* of TNT. In an instant, it was completely obliterated. A vast chasm stood between them and Logan. Even at this distance, Bobbie could see as Logan reacted in utter shock—and then cold, cruel anger.

"You think this will stop me?" he cried, lifting a fist. "All you've done is slow me down!"

Once more, Peg ignored Logan, directing her response to Bobbie and Ben. "Let's hope that slowing him down gives us enough time to do what we need to do. The cure—tell me what it is."

Ben was still in shock over the destruction of the bridge. "We walked across that thing yesterday!" he said. "It could have been blown to bits while we were right in the middle of it!"

"That's true," said Peg. "Good thing I didn't consider you a threat, isn't it?" She turned her focus on Bobbie. "The cure?"

Bobbie hesitated. "Johnny gets the first dose, right? You promise?"

"I promise, dear," said Peg. "Now, if you'd be so kind as to spit it out? We're on a clock."

"We need a golden apple," said Bobbie. "And a Potion of Weakness. Brewed with gunpowder, so we can splash it over him."

Peg nodded, then hurried to the kitchen, where several chests sat against the wall. She began rummaging through them. "I've got the gunpowder. I'll have to prepare the spider eye. And—aha!" She held up an object, and at first it shone so brightly in the sunlight streaming through the windows that Bobbie couldn't see what it was. But Ben gasped, and when Bobbie's vision adjusted, she did the same.

"A golden apple!" Bobbie reached for it, but Peg stashed it away. "I'll hold on to it for now," she said. "Now, I have just about everything I need to get started here. But we will need to delay this Logan person a bit longer. I have a plan for that, but it will require soul sand—and a good amount of it, too."

Bobbie's heart raced. She was so close to curing her brother! If Peg could provide the materials she needed, then she was willing to do anything the woman asked. Peg's quiet confidence made it hard to doubt her, even if she *had* lied about leaving Johnny in Ben's care.

"Where can I find soul sand?" asked Bobbie.

"The soul sand valley," answered Peg. "We saw it during our outing. You remember?"

Bobbie nodded.

"Then go," said Peg. "Hurry, dear! I'll get everything ready here. And I'll keep an eye on our little invader at the same time."

"Okay," Bobbie said. "But Peg . . . one more thing."

Peg looked up impatiently from the open chest. "Yes? What is it?"

"Don't hurt Logan's zombies. They're not responsible for his actions. And . . . if this cure works? Maybe we can save everyone."

Peg smiled. Bobbie wasn't sure why, but the smile looked a little sad to her. "Save everyone, eh, dear? That's very noble of you. But you should focus on one task at a time."

"If you say so. But I'm bringing my team with me." Bobbie grabbed Johnny's lead with one hand and Ben's elbow with the other. "Come on, boys," she said. "I know the way."

"You know the way to a soul sand valley?" asked Ben. "But isn't that in the Nether?" Bobbie nodded, and Ben said, "Wait a minute. You went to the Nether *without me?*"

"Yes. Keep up, Ben!" Bobbie said. Then, tugging on him, she added, "I mean literally, I need you to keep up with me. We've got to get back before Logan makes his way across that chasm!"

CHAPTER 32

"I'm not ready for this."

Ben stood before the Nether portal, which Pigstep Peggy had built in her bedroom (which was weird) and left activated (which seemed reckless). He'd seen portals before. Once, he'd even stood guard at one while Logan ventured within.

But Logan had insisted that the Nether was too dangerous for Ben. He had said that, if they went there together, Ben would get them both killed.

Ever since then, Ben had tried his best to level up—to hone his skills and prove himself a great adventurer! Or at least a competent adventurer.

He thought he would've had more time to prepare.

It didn't help that there was another one of those creepy zombified piglins sniffing around the room.

"Don't mind him," Bobbie said. "That's Shane. He's new."

NICK ELIOPULOS

Ben sighed. "You had an awfully eventful night, didn't you?"

"I did," said Bobbie. "Here, I'll show you." She stepped forward, placing one booted foot on the edge of the portal, and she held out a hand to Ben. "And you *are* ready for this, Ben. It'll be fine. Just follow my lead."

Ben knew she meant to make him feel better. But he could remember a time, not long ago, when she had always followed *his* lead.

Did Bobbie even need him anymore? After all, she'd left him behind—again, and despite her promise not to—to go on an adventure with Pigstep Peggy, who was feeling less like a kindly, gracious host and more like a treacherous captor with each passing hour.

Ben steeled himself, then he followed Bobbie and Johnny through the portal. He half expected to be under attack the moment they emerged, but they were in a forest, and all was quiet and still.

"See? It's not so bad," said Bobbie. Johnny growled, and she laughed. "Don't I take you to the coolest places? Look at those trees! They're not even trees, really. They're mushrooms."

Ben grinned. "Wild," he said, and he felt his nervousness fading. He took a good look all around—

And he accidentally locked eyes with an enderman.

"Oh, slimeballs!" he said.

The enderman made a horrid wailing noise, and then it disappeared.

"Slimeballs!" Ben said. "Run!"

He'd made it only a few steps before the enderman reappeared beside him. It glared at him with furious eyes, lifted its unnaturally long arms, and slammed into him.

Ben went flying off the edge of a cliff. He didn't even have a chance to scream before he landed, hard, on what appeared to be sand.

Ben looked more closely. The sand had . . . *faces* in it. The swirling grains made a perfect picture of a tortured, agonized face.

Now Ben screamed.

"Oh, good!" Bobbie cried from above. "You found the soul sand valley."

"Where's the enderman?" Ben cried. He drew his sword and looked all around. Thanks to the mob's teleportation ability, it could have easily followed him down here.

"I took care of it," Bobbie said. "Look! I got another Ender pearl." She held up a luminous green gem.

Ben knew Ender pearls were very sought after by adventurers, and he felt a stab of jealousy.

And then he felt the stab of an arrow.

"Yeowtch!" he cried, and he wheeled around to see a clutch of skeletons heading his way. Each had a bow raised, and one more arrow struck him before he was able to pull out his shield. A tactical retreat was in order—

But Ben could hardly move. The soul sand was slowing him down. It was like walking through cobwebs. Ben felt a rush of panic at the memory of being helpless in Logan's cobweb trap. He *had* to get out of there.

And then, all of a sudden, Bobbie was running past him,

shield in one hand and sword in the other. The soul sand didn't seem to slow her down at all. She used the very combat technique he had taught her, and with her new sword—was that netherite?—she made it look effortless. The skeletons were vanquished in no time.

"Mawr," complained Johnny. Ben turned to see that the zombie boy had attempted to join the fight, but he was struggling to make his way across the soul sand.

Ben had heard that misery loved company. But he didn't like the idea that he was as useless in a combat encounter as a baby zombie.

Bobbie tossed him an apple. "Here. Are you hurt? I've still got a lot of apples."

"How are you moving so fast?"

She shrugged. "It must be the boots Peg gave me earlier. They're enchanted. She must have realized I might need them here."

"And the sword?" he asked. "She actually gave you a netherite sword?"

"Is that good?" Bobbie asked.

Ben screamed again, this time for entirely different reasons.

"Hey, keep it down!" Bobbie warned. "There are all sorts of weird mobs in this place, and—"

As if to prove her point, a great, ominous squeal sounded from the nearby bastion remnant.

"W-what was that?" asked Ben.

"That's just the piglins," said Bobbie. She began digging up soul sand and placing it in her inventory. "Look, they came out to say hi! Don't worry, they're not hostile."

Ben turned to see a whole crowd of piglins descending from the bastion remnant. Their eyes were locked on Ben, and their golden swords were raised in a threatening manner.

"They . . . do seem sort of hostile, though," he said.

There was some good news, at least—the soul sand slowed the piglins as much as it had slowed Ben. But that hardly balanced the fact that an entire gang of hostile pig-people was coming after him.

"Huh. They seem to have it in for you in particular," said Bobbie.

"Yeah, I noticed," said Ben. "I'm not super popular in the Nether, am I?"

"I think you should run, maybe," said Bobbie.

"I can't run!" Ben said, as he lifted one leaden foot after another.

"Oh, for goodness' sake," said Bobbie, and she placed a series of stone blocks, creating an instant walkway. As soon as Ben clambered onto it, he darted back in the direction of the portal. Along the way, he took a carved pumpkin from his inventory.

"Growr!" said Johnny at the sight of it.

"Don't worry," said Ben. "It's not for you. It's for me! Those endermen mean business."

And if he didn't know better, Ben would have thought he heard the zombie boy laugh as Ben, midstride, plopped the pumpkin onto his own head.

CHAPTER 33

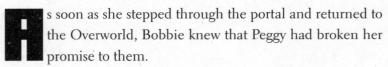s soon as she stepped through the portal and returned to the Overworld, Bobbie knew that Peggy had broken her promise to them.

Shane the zombified piglin was soaking wet, as if just doused with a potion. And Peg was approaching Shane, a golden apple in her hand.

"What are you doing?" cried Bobbie.

Peg glared at Bobbie from over her shoulder. "That was fast. But not fast enough, dear."

As Bobbie watched, Peg fed the golden apple—*Johnny's* golden apple—to Shane.

They all stood there, watching. Bobbie held her breath. Even Johnny seemed to sense that this was a crucial moment.

But the moment passed. Nothing happened.

"It didn't work," Peg said sadly.

"Piglin biology must be too different," Ben guessed.

"Which means you just wasted a cure that we could have given to Johnny!" Bobbie said.

"I can make more," Peg said distractedly. "I'm sure I have all the ingredients around here somewhere."

"We're out of time," said Ben, and he pointed out a nearby window.

From this upper floor, Bobbie had a clear view of the chasm that surrounded Peg's bastion. Logan was nearly done constructing a new bridge. Only it wasn't Logan doing the labor—it was Other Ben. The boy was furiously laying down blocks of stone, crafting a bridge so wide that Logan would be able to march his zombies across it in a great mass of undead bodies.

"I think Other Ben is the key to resolving this," said Bobbie. She turned to face Ben. "Logan is terrible to him. And Other Ben knew I was following them. He could have turned me over to Logan on multiple occasions, and he didn't."

"It's worth a shot," Ben agreed. "I mean, it sort of worked with Hatchet and Flip."

"As for you," said Bobbie, and she turned on Peg, "I thought you were different. But you're just like every other adventurer I've ever met." She tossed the soul sand to the ground. "If you can use this to delay Logan, then use it. Otherwise, I suggest you stay out of our way."

Peg looked guilty. Even her golden armor seemed to shine a little less brightly. "I'll help you," she said. "You want to sneak past Logan and talk to that other boy? Take this."

Ben's jaw dropped open as Peg extended an item toward Bobbie. "Are those what I think they are?" he asked.

"Elytra," confirmed Peg.

Bobbie looked from Peg to Ben and back again. "I don't know what that means," she said.

"They're wings," said Ben. "You can glide through the air with those!"

"Their range is limited," Peg warned. "But they'll get you to the other side of the chasm. I can keep Logan occupied while you talk to the other one."

"How?" asked Ben. "How are you going to stand up to a whole army of zombies?"

"Why, dear, isn't it obvious? After all . . ." Peg grinned darkly. "Logan isn't the only one with an army of zombies at his disposal."

CHAPTER 34

"**A**re you sure about this?" Ben asked.

"Not at all," Bobbie answered. "But we have to try to end this peacefully. And I still think Other Ben is the key to that. I just have to reach him."

"In more ways than one, right?" Ben peered over the ramparts at the lava-filled chasm below and, beyond that, Logan's waiting army, penned in for the moment but sure to be released soon. "Better you than me," he said. "I've always wanted to try elytra, but these aren't exactly the ideal circumstances."

Bobbie turned, showing off the wings she wore on her back. Ben claimed they originated from the End, an even more fearsome dimension than the Nether.

And right now, they were Bobbie's best chance at crossing the chasm unseen and—hopefully—reaching Other Ben before Logan's assault began.

But first, they needed to wait for Peg's distraction.

It would be hard to miss.

As Other Ben placed the final stone block of his bridge, Peg emerged from the bastion. At her back were zombified piglins—*hundreds* of them. They filed out of the structure and onto the makeshift bridge, not so much following Peg as moving about to fill the space. Ben suspected she'd had some of them locked up for a very long time.

"Oy! Logan!" she cried. "You wanted to talk? Let's talk."

"She's got his attention," said Ben. "Now's your chance!"

"Wish me luck," she said, and, climbing atop the ramparts— she jumped.

Bobbie was soaring across the sky! She'd had a lot of new experiences lately, but nothing else compared to the sensation of flying.

Layla reappeared, just in time to join her, flying by her side. Bobbie laughed, enjoying the moment despite the circumstances. But Logan's bridge was complete, and his army would not stay penned in for long. She had to act quickly.

Logan's voice floated up from below. "Pigstep Peggy! Do you remember me?"

"I'm afraid not," answered Peg. "But don't take it personally, dear. Some people simply aren't very memorable."

"How dare you!"

"Just don't look up, Logan," Bobbie mumbled to herself. "Don't look up, don't look up . . ."

He didn't look up, and after a few moments of gliding, Bobbie touched down safely on the far end of the chasm. She crouched low and crept up to the zombie pen. It was a simple wooden fence, just as they'd used to corral the zombies in the subterranean tunnels. Other Ben stood beside it, eyes on Logan and hands gripping an axe. He was clearly waiting for Logan's signal to bring down the fence on one side, which would give the zombies unobstructed access to the bridge.

"Benjamin," she said. "Fancy meeting you here."

Other Ben's eyes went wide as he whirled to face her. "You!" he said. "You're still following us?" He saw Layla hovering beside Bobbie. "And you took the allay—I knew that was you. Why are you hounding us?"

"Because I'm determined to stop Logan. And I think you should help me."

"Me?" said Other Ben. "But I'm Logan's squire!"

"You're his servant," countered Bobbie. "And his punching bag. I've seen how he treats you, Benjamin, and there's no excuse for it."

"It's worth it," Other Ben said. "If he can teach me how to be a great adventurer like him."

"You don't need him for that," said Bobbie. "Look at what I've got."

Bobbie held out her new sword, and Other Ben's mouth dropped open. "Is that *netherite*?" he said, awe in his voice. "And are you wearing *elytra*?"

"My friends and I are pretty successful adventurers, too," said

Bobbie. "So join us. We'll show you the ropes, and we *won't* be jerks about it."

"I can't just abandon him," said Other Ben, but he sounded less certain. "He means well."

"He really doesn't," said Bobbie, and she pulled Logan's journal from her inventory.

"What's that?"

"It's his journal," said Bobbie. "It's where he puts to words what he really thinks." She flipped through its pages. "For example, 'Ben #2 assessment: Useless in combat. Useless at crafting. Above average as zombie bait.'"

"That isn't . . ." said Other Ben. "I don't . . ."

"He goes on to compare you to an axolotl. And if you don't know, he's *not a fan* of axolotls."

Other Ben considered her words for a long moment. His face cycled through a range of emotions. When it landed on *resolved*, Bobbie knew she'd convinced him.

"You're right," said Other Ben. "I don't need Logan."

"That's great," said Bobbie. "You won't regret this, Benjamin. Now here's the plan—"

But Other Ben didn't wait to listen.

"Logan!" he screamed.

"Hey, wait a minute—"

Other Ben wasn't listening to her anymore. He raised his axe.

Logan shouted back, "I'm in the middle of a very ominous monologue right now, Ben!"

"Sorry, Logan, but I'm afraid this can't wait!" shouted Other Ben. "Your army is revolting!"

"Sure, but they've always been pretty gross-looking," said Logan. He chuckled, but when he saw the look on Other Ben's face, his eyes went wide. "Wait, you don't mean—"

"Revolution!" cried Other Ben, and he brought his axe down on the nearest piece of fencing.

Bobbie saw what he was trying to do. Logan was at the midpoint of the bridge, with Peg and her piglins in front of him, and now, an army of zombies at his back. The zombies were "his," but they weren't loyal to him. They would treat him like any other adventurer—in other words, they'd treat him like *breakfast*.

It wasn't a bad plan, Bobbie had to admit. With limited room to maneuver, even Logan wouldn't last forever against a wave of hostile zombies. And if he turned his back on Peg, she would have a golden opportunity to strike him down.

Yes, it was a brilliant move—if you didn't care how many of the zombies were destroyed in the process.

But Bobbie cared very much.

"No!" she cried. "Stop! We can end this peacefully."

But it was too late. The first wave of zombies was already approaching Logan. "Ben, you fool!" he cried. "You'll pay for this."

The zombies moved quickly, but Logan was quicker. He ducked the first blow—and the zombie struck a zombified piglin by accident.

The zombified piglin squealed in rage, and its anger seemed to spread throughout the assembled creatures.

"Oh no," Bobbie said, in the instant before chaos broke out.

It was war now. A war between zombies and zombified pig-lins.

And Bobbie feared that none of them would make it out alive.

CHAPTER 35

Ben looked down on a scene of carnage and chaos, the likes of which he'd never seen before.

Zombified piglins were attacking zombies. Zombies were hitting zombified piglins. Logan was striking out at anything that got within reach. Pigstep Peggy was howling with despair each time a piglin was struck. Bobbie was at the back of the zombie horde, dropping blocks to trap as many zombie villagers as she could. Other Ben was waving his axe around and shouting insults at Logan, some of which were almost enough to make Ben blush.

Bobbie's plan to drive a wedge between Logan and Other Ben had clearly worked a little *too* well.

At Ben's shoulder, Johnny grunted.

"You want in on the big battle?" Ben asked. "Well, forget it. That's the kind of fight that *nobody* wins."

All the same, Ben needed to do something. If he knew Bobbie, she'd be throwing herself into the fray, all in an effort to prevent her zombified neighbors from getting injured. And between Logan's sword and the piglins' claws, some of those neighbors were definitely going to take some damage.

Ben realized that was how he could help. He couldn't prevent the damage from occurring. But with the right potions, he could heal the zombies before they were destroyed. Ben laughed at his brilliance . . .

Then he groaned at the realization that he was actually planning to *heal* blood-crazed, undead hostile mobs. Things had been a lot simpler before he'd met Bobbie and Johnny, that was for sure.

Ben rushed downstairs to the series of chests Peg had set up near her brewing stand. There were plenty of potions on hand— including the dark purple Potions of Harming he was looking for, and copious gunpowder, which he could use to make them into splash potions.

While the potions were brewing, he checked the other chests for anything else that could help with the battle. And that's when Ben saw something that set his heart to soaring.

Peg had gold ingots. She had a *lot* of gold ingots.

Ben had always loved the look of gold, the way it glittered. It wasn't as nice as emeralds, but it was plenty nice!

These days, however, gold had a whole new value. Combined with the apple that Bobbie had given him in the Nether . . .

He could craft the golden apple they needed to cure Johnny!

Just then, the front door slammed open, and Pigstep Peggy stormed into the bastion.

"I can explain!" Ben said, stepping away from the open chest.

"I don't care what you take," Peg said. "It's all gone wrong. All my plans—my hopes for a piglin utopia here in the Overworld—reduced to ash." Peg leveled him with a darkly intense look. "No, I don't care what you take," she said. "So long as you leave the Wither skulls to me."

Ben didn't love the sound of that, but then, he hadn't much liked Peg from the start. "She trusted you, you know," he said to her now. "Bobbie did. And it takes a lot for her to trust an adventurer. She saw right through the Overlords. She saw through *me*, when we first met—she could see how I was motivated by all the wrong things, and she showed me a better way. Her compassion makes the Overworld a better place, and you used it against her."

"It's easy to be compassionate when you're young," said Peg as she rummaged through the chest of bones. "But this world disappoints all of us in the end. I just helped your friend grow up a little. Now, if you'll excuse me, Logan appears to have the upper hand out there, and if I'm going down, it's going to be in a blaze of glory that will have people talking for *years*."

"It won't come to that," said Ben. "We've beaten him before. We'll beat him again."

Peg paused her looting to look over her shoulder and raise an eyebrow. "I thought you were the suspicious, worldly one. But it seems like your naïve friend is rubbing off on you."

"I hope you're right," Ben said. "And she needs me out there!" Moving quickly, he gathered the splash potion he'd been brewing and then turned to a crafting table, where he combined one apple and eight gold ingots. In no time at all, he held a golden apple in his hands. Finally!

Ben steeled himself for the chaos, and then he ran out the door and into the fray. If anything, the scene was more chaotic at ground level than it had appeared from up above. As he watched, a zombie villager suffered a brutal attack from its piglin opponent. Ben wasted no time, tossing a Potion of Harming at the zombie villager, ensuring that it wouldn't be destroyed. As an undead mob, the zombie would have found a healing potion toxic, but the harming potion quickly undid the piglin's damage.

Ben worked his way through the crowd, tossing potions as he went. With the undead mobs pulling so much aggro, he was attacked only a few times, and he found it easy enough to duck the attacks and lose himself in the crowd. Eventually, he made his way to Bobbie.

"What are you doing?" she asked.

"I'm keeping your neighbors from being destroyed! Thank me later," he said. "But you can thank me *now* for this." He held out the golden apple.

Bobbie's eyes went wide. Then she lunged forward, wrapping her arms around him. "Ben, you're amazing!" The allay chirped happily.

"I know, I know," he said. Then, as Bobbie pulled out of their embrace, she took the apple with her off hand and knocked back an attacking piglin with her sword. Ben laughed. "You're not so bad yourself. But we need a way to stop this mess."

"It looks like Peg might have an idea," Bobbie said. "Look."

Ben turned to see Peg building something right at the base of her bastion. What had she said a few minutes ago? Something about a blaze of glory?

"Oh no," Ben said. "I think I know what she's making."

"What?" asked Bobbie. "What is it?"

"No time!" said Ben. "We have to stop her now!"

Ben tried to hurry. But there were so many bodies between them and Peggy. He dodged a zombie's swipe attack as Peg placed a final piece of soul sand. He slashed at an attacking piglin as she set the first Wither skull in place atop the sand.

And then, suddenly, Logan loomed before him.

"You!" he said, and his eyes hopped from Ben to Bobbie. "And you! I should have known you'd be here. Don't you ever get tired of messing with me?"

"Yell at us later," said Ben. "But let us pass now! Don't you see what Peggy is building?"

As Ben said the words, Peg put a second Wither skull in position.

"She couldn't be that reckless," said Logan. "She wouldn't build a Wither on her own doorstep, would she?"

But as the trio watched, Pigstep Peggy did just that. With the addition of a third and final skull, her build shuddered to life.

Ben grabbed his crossbow. "We need to strike now!" he said. "Before it's fully awake!"

He began peppering the mob with arrows. Peg noticed right away. She looked up at them, a mournful look in her eyes.

"It's too late," said Peg. "It's all gone wrong. This Wither will erase my mistakes here—and all of you." She shook her head. "I'm done with the Overworld. I'm going to the Nether, and this time, I'm never coming back."

Logan shot an arrow from his bow. It lodged into her armor, and Peg scowled. "A brat until the end, aren't you?"

"Logan!" shouted Ben. "Shoot the Wither, not the old woman, you big llama. We're running out of time." Yet Ben's arrows seemed to have no effect on the Wither, which was growing larger with each passing second.

"It can't be hurt until it explodes," said Logan.

"Explodes?" Bobbie's eyes went wide. "Peg, don't do this!" she cried. "We can still end this peaceful—"

The Wither exploded as it awakened, partially obliterating the bridge as it came fully into its power. Peg, distracted by Logan's attack, hadn't gotten far enough away. The old adventurer was thrown off the crumbling ledge and into the chasm below. Zombies and piglins followed Peg, toppling into the lava.

"No!" cried Bobbie.

But there was nothing any of them could do.

The Wither rose into the air. It shrieked . . . and it turned its three sinister faces onto them.

CHAPTER 36

As a rule, Bobbie wasn't eager to follow Logan's commands. But when the boy yelled, "Scatter!" she didn't think twice.

Bobbie fought her way back across the bridge. She left her sword in her inventory, using only her fists, still reluctant to cause any major damage to the zombies that surrounded her. Even so, she found herself punching and slapping, forcing the mobs away from her in a desperate scramble to get off the bridge.

The Wither was tossing skulls, seemingly at random, and they exploded on impact. Another piece of the bridge was blown to bits, mere blocks away from Bobbie. She screamed, ducked her head, and kept moving.

The next skull was even closer. It blasted poor Layla right out of the air. Bobbie felt her heart breaking at the sight, but it was all over before she could do anything. She had thought the gentle mob couldn't be hurt—none of the zombies had seemed to even notice her. But the Wither was more powerful—and more evil—than anything she'd fought before.

Other Ben stood at the far side of the bridge, on solid ground, where Bobbie wouldn't have to worry about the floor being blown out from under her. He extended a hand to her.

"Come on!" said Other Ben. "You're almost there. You can make it!"

It happened so fast. One second, Other Ben was there, hand outstretched, cheering her on.

The next second, a skull fell at his feet, exploding on impact.

Other Ben flew back, landing at the base of the nearby mountain. It had been nearly a direct hit; he didn't look good.

Bobbie wasted no time. She swung her diamond pickaxe against the mountain face, carving a small cavern for shelter, then she dragged Other Ben inside.

"Are you okay?" asked Bobbie. "Where does it hurt?"

"E-everywhere," said Other Ben, wincing.

"Serves him right," said Logan, who came to stand beside them. "This whole mess is his fault."

"Now's not the time for blame," Bobbie snapped. "And where is my Ben?"

"He ran the other way," Logan answered. "Into the bastion."

Other Ben coughed.

"He's got Wither," Logan said. "He's a goner, unless you have any milk."

"I—I don't," Bobbie said, frantically combing through her inventory. "Just apples. And this!"

She held up the golden apple.

Logan whistled. "That might do the trick. If it helps him regenerate health faster than the withering drains it."

"But . . . but I need it," Bobbie said. "It's for my brother."

"Suit yourself," Logan said, and he chuckled. "You're not as soft as I thought. Maybe you've got what it takes to be an adventurer after all. You could join what's left of the Overworld Overlords."

Logan meant it as a compliment, but his words were revolting to Bobbie. And they brought her back to her senses. She could never let someone else suffer—not if she had the power to help.

She fed the golden apple to Other Ben. He seemed to feel better immediately. "That . . . that was amazing," he said. "I can feel it working!"

"That's good," Bobbie said. "But keep your voice down. That thing is still out there . . ."

She peered out the cave and watched as the Wither scanned the area for new targets. It didn't seem interested in attacking the zombified mobs all around it, and the piglins and zombies had stopped fighting each other, too. It looked like one great, big happy undead family out there.

Bobbie saw some familiar faces among the horde. Her neighbors had survived the carnage, and they were right there, almost close enough to reach! But she didn't dare try anything while the Wither floated menacingly above them.

Her neighbors were still lost to her. For now.

EPILOGUE

The Wither hadn't attacked any of the undead mobs, which Logan found fascinating. He was already wondering if there was some way to use that to his advantage. A Wither at the head of his zombie army? That would be the stuff of legends!

But then Logan remembered: He didn't *have* a zombie army anymore. His soldiers had scattered in every direction once the Wither had blown a few holes through the volcano. And since they were wearing iron helmets, the sunlight wouldn't affect them. They could go pretty much anywhere.

Logan sighed. It would be a lot of hard work to round them up again. And Logan didn't love hard work.

Still, he came out of the disaster better than anybody else. Pigstep Peggy had almost definitely perished in the lava below, so *technically*, he'd accomplished what he came here to do. And he saw the girl, Bobbie, shed a few tears for an allay that had been following her around.

Logan moved a little closer to hear what Ben and Bobbie were saying to each other.

"I don't like it," Ben said to Bobbie.

"What's to like?" Bobbie replied. "Look around you, Ben. This was apocalyptic."

Logan took another look around. Peg's bastion was a remnant of its former glory. The wide stone bridge where the battle had taken place was nothing but shattered fragments of stone. Craters pockmarked the soil where the Wither's explosive skulls had landed.

Their pet zombie groaned, and the sound made the scene only seem bleaker.

"And this was only the beginning," Bobbie continued. "That Wither flew off, and two undead armies went with it. They're roaming the countryside, a deadly danger to anyone they come across."

"And even the sunlight won't keep people safe from those zombies," Ben said. "Thanks to *him*."

Logan scowled. "It was a brilliant plan, and you know it." He crossed his arms. "But even I have to admit that things have gotten out of hand. I want riches and fame. Power! If the Overworld gets trampled and scorched, that doesn't help me." He grinned. "But beating a Wither? That would be *pretty good* for my reputation."

Other Ben frowned at Logan. "Well, maybe you don't feel responsible for all this, but I do." He turned to the others. "I'll do anything I can to help fix this."

Logan scoffed. "Anything *you* can do isn't going to be very much help."

"That's enough!" Bobbie said sharply. "If this is going to have any hope of working, we have to support each other. We have to at least try."

"So your mind is made up?" asked Ben. "We're really doing this?"

"We're really doing this." Bobbie extended a hand. "Logan. Benjamin. Welcome to the team."

The zombie kid grumbled, and Ben did, too.

But Logan laughed. "Welcome to *my* team, you mean," he said, and he squeezed Bobbie's hand hard as he shook it. "Follow my lead . . . do *everything* I say . . ." Logan grinned darkly. "And you might all survive this adventure after all."

ACKNOWLEDGMENTS

Sequels are hard, but any opportunity to build something new in the world of Minecraft is (as any kid knows) a tremendous honor. I remain so grateful to the folks at Mojang who have given me so much freedom to play in their infinite sandbox. A special thank-you to Alex Wiltshire, whose insights and creativity have helped me to avoid many a plot hole and pitfall.

The grace, wisdom, and imagination of my editor, Elizabeth Schaefer, remain unmatched. She has such a keen eye for the character moments that make or break a story, and it makes my job much easier to know she has such affection for these characters and their journey. Thank you, Elizabeth!

My sincere thanks also to the rest of the Penguin Random House crew, including Alex Davis, Elizabeth A. D. Eno, and the many, many talented folks who work tirelessly to produce books that kids will cherish.

Thanks to my agents, Josh and Tracey Adams, who would have my back even in a zombie apocalypse.

Thanks to my husband, Andrew, who is happy to spend a cozy writing weekend indoors, and to our beloved new cat, Bentley, who only occasionally steps on my laptop.

Thanks to my Monday lunch crew, Billy and David and Zack, who make sure I take a proper break every now and then.

Thanks to my brother, Jason (who loves zombies), and my sister, Lindsay (who loves llamas). And to my dad, who brags about these books. And to my mom, who was visiting while I was revising this novel. She made sure I was well fed while I worked!

Thanks to all the kids and parents who write me letters. I cherish every one of them.

And one last, very special shout-out, to the local librarians who have been so welcoming as I've moved to a new area and started building new personal and professional connections from scratch. Librarians are the heart and soul of any community, and the ones I've met over the last year have made it obvious that I've found a great home. Thank you for all that you do!

ABOUT THE AUTHOR

NICK ELIOPULOS is a professional writer, editor, game designer, and teacher. (He likes to keep busy.) He is the author of two officially licensed Minecraft chapter book series, the Woodsword Chronicles and the Stonesword Saga, as well as the co-author of The Adventurers Guild Trilogy. Nick was born in Florida, lives in New York, and spends most of his free time in the Nether.

ABOUT THE TYPE

This book was set in Electra, a typeface designed for Linotype by W. A. Dwiggins, the renowned type designer (1880–1956). Electra is a fluid typeface, avoiding the contrasts of thick and thin strokes that are prevalent in most modern typefaces.

DISCOVER MORE MINECRAFT
HAVE YOU READ THEM ALL?

- [ ] *The Island* by Max Brooks
- [ ] *The Crash* by Tracey Baptiste
- [ ] *The Lost Journals* by Mur Lafferty
- [ ] *The End* by Catherynne M. Valente
- [ ] *The Voyage* by Jason Fry
- [ ] *The Rise of the Arch-Illager* by Matt Forbeck
- [ ] *The Shipwreck* by C. B. Lee
- [ ] *The Mountain* by Max Brooks
- [ ] *The Dragon* by Nicky Drayden
- [ ] *Mob Squad* by Delilah S. Dawson
- [ ] *The Haven Trials* by Suyi Davies
- [ ] *Mob Squad: Never Say Nether* by Delilah S. Dawson
- [ ] *Zombies!* by Nick Eliopulos
- [ ] *Mob Squad: Don't Fear the Creeper* by Delilah S. Dawson
- [ ] *Castle Redstone* by Sarwat Chadda

Penguin
Random
House

DISCOVER MORE MINECRAFT

LEVEL UP YOUR GAME WITH THE OFFICIAL GUIDES

MORE MINECRAFT:

Penguin
Random
House